Kelpies is an imprint of Floris Books

First published in 2016 by Floris Books
© 2016 Robert J. Harris

The publisher acknowledges subsidy from
Creative Scotland towards the publication
of this volume

 This book is also
available as an eBook

British Library CIP data available
ISBN 978-178250-262-3
Printed & Bound by MBM Print SCS Ltd, Glasgow

# Robert J. Harris

*To my mum and dad,*
*for all the adventures they let me have.*

# 1. An Unexpected Forest

As the 95A bus pulled out of St Andrews bus station on its way to Dundee, teenagers Greg McBride and Susie Spinetti were having an argument.

"You know your problem, Spinny?" Greg declared in disgust. "You're unsophisticated."

"Sorry, Greg," said Susie, handing back his iPod, "I just can't get into this stuff. What did you say his name was again? Rod Kestrel?"

"*Rawkestra*," Greg corrected her sharply. "They're only the most awesome metal band on the planet, and their album *Running from the Jaguar* is a total beast."

"It's a total something," Susie agreed. "Have you not got any good bands, like Black and White Rainbow or Arguments with the satnav?"

"Oh right, like I'd listen to that rubbish." Greg bit a chunk off his chocolate bar like that put an end to the conversation.

"You know, if we could find music we both enjoyed," Susie sighed, "it would be good for our relationship."

"Relationship!" Greg nearly choked on his chocolate. "Spinny, we do not have a relationship. We're pals, okay?"

Susie shrugged. "If you say so, Greg."

There were over a dozen passengers on the bus and Greg and Susie were seated near the back, on their way to the Olympia swimming pool in Dundee. As the bus moved down City Road, Greg stifled a yawn and flicked through the tracks on his iPod. He finally selected 'Red Fire on a Blue, Blue Night', which had an epic solo by the band's Hungarian bassist Giorgio Pips.

"You've been yawning ever since we got on the bus," said Susie. "Good thing we're going for a splash in the pool. That'll wake you up."

"Could you not have let me sleep a bit longer before you came banging on the door at the crack of dawn?" Greg complained.

"Half past nine isn't the crack of dawn," Susie pointed out. "I've been up since seven."

"That's because you're clinically overactive. When you're not playing hockey, you're swimming. When you're not swimming, you're playing football. When you're not playing football—"

"I'm goofing around with you," Susie laughed, giving him a playful thump on the shoulder. "Where are you getting all these big words from anyway? Did you have dictionary-on-toast for breakfast?"

Greg pulled a second-hand paperback out of his pocket. "I'm getting them from this."

"You, a book?" said Susie sceptically. "Has it got a lot of pictures in it?"

"Only a few," said Greg, "by way of *illustration*."

Susie took the book and read the cover. "*THE VERBAL NINJA: How to Make People Do What You Want by Using the Right Words.*"

"It will help me in my future careers," said Greg. "I've decided it's time to start thinking about my future."

"And what careers would those be?" Susie asked, flipping through the pages. "Zookeeper? Gameshow host?"

Greg counted off on his fingers in what he thought was a businesslike manner. "First fighter pilot, then advertising executive, then," he concluded grandly, "president."

"President?" said Susie. "This is Scotland. We don't have a president."

"Not yet," said Greg with a grin. "I'll be the first."

"Does Lewis know you're reading a book?" asked Susie. "I'm surprised it's not in all the papers."

Greg's younger brother Lewis was very serious-minded and rarely had his nose out of a book.

"He wouldn't notice if I'd taken up fire-eating," Greg scoffed. "For weeks he's been daft on fish. He's bought himself a pair of goldfish and today he's off to the harbour to catch a piranha."

"He's not going to catch a piranha in St Andrews," Susie chuckled.

"Well, he's off to catch something," said Greg. "I wasn't really listening."

Susie returned the book and Greg stuffed it back in his pocket.

"So are you going to use your new Jedi mind powers to make me do what you want?" she asked impishly.

"There's an easier way to do that," said Greg. He pulled out a chocolate and raisin cereal bar and passed it to her.

"Hey, cool!" said Susie, stripping off the wrapper and taking a big bite. "Thanks!" she said through a mouthful of chocolate and raisins.

Greg wriggled down in his seat and closed his eyes. "Now pipe down and let me sleep."

It was a bright October day and the morning sun flashed off the wide windows of the university science buildings to their left. Off to the right, beyond the playing fields and the golf course, the waters of St Andrews Bay lapped against the West Sands.

The bus was just passing the entrance to Baldrovie Farm when there was a sudden lurch as the driver slammed on the brakes.

"Oh great!" Greg groused as he was jolted forward. "Can't a guy get any peace?" He kept his eyes firmly closed and squirmed back into a comfortable sleeping position.

Susie stood up and peered ahead through the driver's windscreen. "Greg, you need to see this," she gasped.

"It's not a sheep in the road again, is it?" said Greg, reluctantly opening his eyes.

There was a buzz among the passengers and they were all peering out the windows.

"Here, have you taken a wrong turn?" one woman demanded of the driver.

"Aye, it looks like we're in the middle of Tentsmuir Forest," said another.

"We've not gone that far," said Susie. "If you look back you can still see the Old Course Hotel."

"That lassie's right," somebody agreed. "What on earth is going on?"

Greg could see what the fuss was about. They were only a short distance out of town and the Dundee road should have been stretching in front of them. Instead a line of tall, dark trees was spread right across the road. In fact, a dense, wild-looking forest sprawled as far as the eye could see, all the way down to the coast.

A few other cars pulled up behind the bus. Faced

with the obstacle ahead, the drivers, one by one, turned around and headed back to town.

"I'll bet it's got something to do with they GM crops," an old man declared darkly.

"Come on, Spinny, we need to get a look at this," said Greg.

"You're right," Susie agreed as they made their way down the aisle to the front of the bus.

The driver was on his radio trying to contact the bus station, and getting only static in reply. "Back in your seats, please," he said when he saw them coming.

"We need to get outside," said Greg.

"Out?" echoed the driver. "No, you don't. There's something right queer going on and I'm taking no chances. We're headed straight back to the station."

"Look, Susie here swears she saw her granny out there wandering through the trees," Greg explained, placing a sympathetic hand on Susie's shoulder.

"Her granny?" The driver frowned. "What would her granny be doing out there in the trees?"

"Grannies are always getting lost in the woods," said Greg, sounding like an expert on the subject of lost grannies. "Did you never hear about Red Riding Hood's granny?"

Susie gave the driver a wide-eyed look, like a worried kitten. "Please, mister. My granny's not well.

I'm scared something'll happen to her if we don't fetch her inside."

"Okay," said the driver unhappily, twisting the lever to open the door. "Mind you're only a minute, though, then we're heading back."

Greg and Susie hopped down and walked towards the tree line.

"Red Riding Hood's granny didn't get lost in the woods," said Susie. "She got eaten by a wolf."

"Fine, you're such an expert, you go back and tell him that," said Greg, jerking a thumb back at the bus.

They halted a short distance from the forest and stared. The trees were as high as a five-storey building with leaves of such a dark green they looked almost black. Now and again they glimpsed a shadowy form slipping through the mysterious woodland and they could hear rustles, snorts and crackles.

"This is totally... I don't know... it's totally *something*," said Greg.

"I'll bet there's a word for it in that book of yours," said Susie. "Do you think it's got anything to do with... you know... Loki?"

"It's his style alright," said Greg. He shook his head. "You'd think he'd be fed up of messing about with St Andrews by now."

Once before, Loki, the Viking god of magic and

mischief, had turned St Andrews into a mad fantasy world of ogres and goblins. Then another time he buried the town under a torrent of snow right in the middle of summer.

"But did Odin not say he tossed him into some dark hole way beyond the edge of time and space?" said Susie, recalling how their last adventure with the Norse gods had ended.

"It did sound pretty foolproof," Greg agreed, rubbing a hand through his unruly thatch of brown hair. "I suppose there could be something else going on."

"Maybe it's aliens who want to use the Earth to supply them with timber," Susie suggested. "They might have developed a strain of fast-growing trees."

Greg suddenly raised his right hand. "Spinny, is your finger tingling?"

"It is!" Susie exclaimed. "What's going on?"

They both stared at the rings they were wearing. Forged from Asgardian gold and marked with a bolt of lightning, Odin had given the rings to Greg, Susie and Greg's younger brother Lewis, to thank them for their help defeating Loki. Now the rings were vibrating and a tingling sensation ran down their fingers and right up their arms.

All of a sudden it stopped.

As Greg and Susie stared at each other in surprise,

the driver's voice sounded out behind them, "Come on, you kids! Get back on board!"

"What's his hurry?" Greg grumbled. "It's not like it's a long way back to the bus station."

"I think he's right, Greg," Susie breathed. "Look!"

An immense animal was emerging from the dark shadow of the trees. She could see it was covered in thick, black bristles and its small, hostile eyes glared at them down the length of two vicious tusks.

"It's some kind of pig," said Greg, taking a step back, "except three times the size."

"More like a wild boar," said Susie. "And I think it's looking for a fight."

With a wicked gleam in its piggy eyes the boar advanced on them. When Susie and Greg backed off it scraped the tarmac with its front trotters and let out an angry squeal. It was about to charge when the bus driver sounded a loud blast on his horn that stopped it in its tracks.

"Back to the bus, Spinny!" Greg urged.

He grabbed Susie by the shoulder to turn her around and they both pelted full speed for the bus. They heard an angry snort and a clatter of hooves as the boar lumbered after them.

The doors opened with a hiss and they leapt inside. As the doors closed behind them, the boar scored a huge gash in the bus' paintwork with one of its tusks, prompting cries of alarm from the passengers.

"I hope your granny's not really out there," the driver said as Susie and Greg flopped into the seat behind him.

"If she was, she'd turn that thing into a pile of bacon rolls," said Susie. "She used to work on a farm."

Muttering some nasty words under his breath, the driver threw the bus into reverse. The boar wheeled around and charged, this time colliding head-on with the radiator grille and bouncing back.

"Clear off, you mad beast!" the driver yelled. He had one eye on the boar and another on the rear-view mirror as he continued to reverse at top speed.

The animal stopped and glowered at the bus as it reversed up a small farm road then turned back towards St Andrews. After the vehicle roared off, the boar let out a squeal of triumph, clearly deciding it had won this fight by a knockout.

Everybody on the bus chattered excitedly, totally baffled as to what was going on.

"If Loki's surrounded the town with that dark forest..." said Susie.

"We're trapped," Greg said with a grim nod.

# 2. Dave the Lobster

Greg's younger brother Lewis didn't know anything about the scary forest that had just appeared on the edge of town. He was down at St Andrews harbour, carefully lowering an empty glass jar on the end of a length of string into the water. His tongue was sticking out of the right side of his mouth, like it often did when he was concentrating.

He ignored the noise of the fishermen unloading their catch, the cawing of the gulls hovering about in search of scraps, and the chatter of some students who were taking a stroll down the pier in their bright red gowns. Here and there people were walking their dogs or just taking in the sea air.

"Hey there, mate, what's that you're up to?" a voice hailed him. "You'll never catch a lobster in that jam jar. It's way too small."

Startled, Lewis looked up and saw Dave the Lobster walking towards him.

Dave the Lobster was not actually a lobster.

He just knew a lot about them. He was doing research in marine biology at St Andrews University and he had come to the high school a couple of weeks ago to give a talk – about lobsters, of course.

Their teacher had introduced him to Lewis' class as Mr David Eccles from the Gatty Marine Laboratory, but by the time he'd spent an hour talking about lobsters, everyone was referring to him as Dave the Lobster.

As he ambled towards Lewis with his hands in his pockets, Dave the Lobster's spiky hair was pointing straight up at the sky, the way hair does in cartoons when people get a fright. He was wearing a t-shirt with a picture of a lobster playing the guitar and the words 'Rock Lobster'.

"Oh, hello, Mr Eccles," said Lewis.

"Never mind that Mr Eccles lark," said Dave the Lobster with a grin. "Just call me Dave. Hey, I remember you from the school. You were the one that asked all those questions about plankton and stuff."

"That's right, I'm..."

"No, don't tell me," Dave interrupted. "I never forget a face or a name. Well, I might forget one, but I never forget both. It starts with an 'L', right? It's... Elvis?"

"It's Lewis actually."

"Close enough, eh? So what are you up to, Elvis?"

Lewis didn't bother correcting him again. "I'm taking

a water sample so I can examine it for marine life," he explained.

Dave the Lobster's eyebrows shot up. "Whoa! Been bitten by the marine science bug, have you? I know what that's like. When I was three I caught a tadpole in the pond behind my house. I was so excited I fell in. Took my mum ages to dry me off and she had to give me a jammy biscuit to stop me wailing. Didn't put me off science, though."

Lewis looked down to where the jar was floating in the harbour. He had to tug on the string to tilt it so that it would fill with water and sink. After a couple of tugs it plopped down out of sight.

"I can tell you what you're going to find," said Dave the Lobster. "Crab larvae, diatoms, some copepods and, oh yeah, loads of fish eggs. There are fish eggs floating about all over the sea, millions of them. Of course, you'll need a microscope to see them. Got one?"

"A fish egg?"

"No, a microscope."

"Yes, I got one for my birthday," said Lewis as he hauled the jar back up. Holding it in his hand, he peered at it and a puzzled frown appeared on his face.

"Hang on," said Dave the Lobster, leaning in for a look, "that's a bit weird."

Instead of being green and muddy, the water in the jar was a clear, light blue. It sparkled in the sunlight.

"Are you practising some kind of magic trick?" asked Dave the Lobster. "If you are, it's a good one."

"No," said Lewis, shaking his head. "This is straight out of the harbour."

Dave the Lobster's jaw worked from side to side as if he were chewing on the problem. "Maybe there's been some kind of chemical spill."

Lewis peered out across the bay and saw a white mist drifting in from the sea. "Could that cause mist as well?" he asked.

Dave followed Lewis' gaze and his jaw worked even harder. "Tell you what," he suggested, "empty out the jar and take a fresh sample. Maybe that first one was just a fluke."

They both stared down and saw that the water directly below them was the same as in the jar – a bright, clear blue.

"I don't think it will make any difference," said Lewis.

At that moment the students who were standing out on the very end of the pier yelled excitedly. They were pointing out to sea, where a dragon's head with huge red eyes had just poked out of the mist.

Their squeals turned to laughter and relief when they saw that the dragon's head and neck were both made of wood. It was the prow of a ship that now surged fully into view.

"That's a pretty old-style boat," Dave the Lobster observed.

"It's a Viking longship," said Lewis.

The ship was long and sleek with two banks of oars rapidly chopping the water. With the dragonhead leading the way, it sped across the waves like a skimming stone.

"They're going at some lick!" Dave exclaimed. "Those boys must be rowing like the clappers."

"And they're coming right for us," said Lewis.

The heads of the crew bowed and bobbed as they leaned forward and hauled back on the oars. Lewis was sure there was something strange about the rowers but he couldn't make out any details at this distance. He felt a tingle down his spine, an instinctive warning of danger. He'd had plenty of experience with Viking magic and it always meant trouble.

"I've got it," said Dave the Lobster. "It must be some kind of historical re-enactment, you know, like all that Viking malarkey they do up in Shetland."

"We're a long way from Shetland," Lewis pointed out.

"Yeah, well, I expect they got lost in that fog," said Dave. "They should have used satnav."

As the speeding ship reached the harbour mouth,

the excited cries of the students turned to gasps of horror. They turned tail and dashed back towards town with their gowns flapping about their legs.

Dave the Lobster shouted after them, "It's alright! They're not real Vikings!" He turned to Lewis with a laugh and said, "Honestly, you'd think students would have a bit more sense."

"They're maybe not as daft as you think." Lewis gulped.

As the ship pulled up alongside the pier, he could now see that the crew weren't human. They were wolves.

One of them tied the ship to a metal ring on the pier wall then they all filed up the stone stairway, walking on their hind legs. They wore shirts of chainmail, and each had a sword hanging at their side.

They lined up along the pier and made an attempt to stand to attention like soldiers on guard. However, they remained hunched, ready to spring on unwary prey, ears alert for danger and teeth bared in a threatening snarl.

The next figure to climb out of the longship was normal in comparison. From his red hair and small, pointed beard, his bright green suit and matching hat, you would have taken him for an overdressed businessman or a Las Vegas gambler.

Lewis recognised him at once as Loki, the Viking god of magic and mischief. His first impulse was to run away. His second impulse was to run away even faster. However, he knew he had to hang around to find out what the villain was up to this time.

Loki snapped his fingers and the wolf creatures fell into line behind him as he strolled up the pier, surveying the harbour as if he owned the place. The students had disappeared from sight but here and there passers-by were gathering in knots to stare at the strange new arrivals.

Flanked by his wolf guards, Loki stepped off the pier onto the harbour path.

"Wow those costumes are mega-cool!" Dave the Lobster exclaimed. "You'd almost think they were real wolves. Hey, do you think they could make me a lobster costume for the Marine Science Department's Halloween party?"

"Dave, I don't think this is any sort of re-enactment," said Lewis.

"Oh, right," said Dave with a grin. "They're making a *movie*." He glanced around eagerly. "Can't see any cameras. They must have them hidden so they don't spoil the shot."

Lewis realised the Viking god had spotted him. It was too late to run.

Loki sauntered up to him with the wolves close behind. "Well, well, look who's here," he said with a smirk.

"On your own this time, eh, squirt? Where's that loudmouth brother of yours and that feisty girl?"

Lewis swallowed hard. "They're out of town for the day." He knew Greg would have come up with a snappier answer so he added, "Not that it's any of your business."

"Lucky for them, eh?" Loki chuckled. "But not so much for you."

"Say, Elvis, do you know this guy?" asked Dave the Lobster.

Loki raised a scornful eyebrow. "And who is this clown?"

"Dave the Lobster," Lewis answered without thinking. "Sorry, Mr Eccles," he apologised. "That's what everybody at school calls you."

"No, it's cool," Dave beamed. "Dave the Lobster. Yeah, I like it." He turned to Loki and offered a handshake. "And who might you be? All dressed up for St Patrick's Day, are you? You're a bit late."

Loki ignored the outstretched hand. "I am Loki," he answered with an arrogant sneer. "Lord Loki, absolute ruler of this run-down burg—"

"Hey, no need to diss the town," Dave interrupted.

Loki scowled and pressed on. "Ruler of this burg and all that lies beyond." With a sweep of his arm he indicated all the countryside around St Andrews.

"That's a nice suit," Dave the Lobster complimented him, "and I like the hat too. Could I try it on? I always fancied myself in a trilby."

"It's not a trilby, it's a fedora," Loki snapped.

"Alright, keep your hair on. I was only asking," said Dave. He turned his attention to one of the guards. "That's pretty neat make-up, Logan. What are they supposed to be? Werewolves?"

"They're wolflings," Loki informed him testily, "children of Fenris the Great Wolf."

Dave let out a low whistle to show how impressed he was. "So all this, the ship and everything, is this a publicity stunt for your movie or are you filming now with secret cameras?"

"This isn't a film, you chump," Loki barked. "I'm taking over. Get it? I've done away with Asgard, Odin and all the rest, and I've grabbed this little town of yours like it was a piece of candy."

Dave scratched his head. "I'm not sure I follow you, Logan. Have you got a hand-out or something you could give me?"

The wolf guards growled and Dave took a step back. Lewis had a feeling he'd better distract the god of mischief before the wolves turned Dave into a snack.

"Look, Loki, it's only a matter of time before Thor or Odin comes along to pound on you," he said, trying to sound reasonable. "So why don't you give it up now and save everybody a lot of grief?"

Loki gave an evil chuckle. "Don't hold your breath waiting for any of those jokers to show up."

Lewis' heart sank. If the other gods didn't appear, and with Greg and Susie off to Dundee, it would be up to him to find a way to stop the god of mischief. He was wondering what on earth he could possibly do when he heard the sound of a car engine.

A police car appeared from behind the fishermen's cottages, honking its horn to clear people out of the way.

"Hey, the cops!" Dave the Lobster exclaimed with a grin. "Don't you worry, Elvis. They'll sort this out."

"It will take more than a caution to deal with Loki," said Lewis, "and arresting him could be tricky."

# 3. Bird of Prey

There were murmurs of both amazement and annoyance among the passengers as the bus drove back into town and up City Road.

Greg pulled out his phone. "I need to call Lewis and warn him," he explained.

"Good idea," said Susie. "Maybe he'll have some idea what's going on."

Greg dialled a number. Instead of a ring, a chorus of high-pitched voices squeaked painfully. He pulled the phone away and stared at it as if it had just bitten him. "Great!" he groaned, switching it off. "The road's blocked and my phone's gone nuts. Try yours."

"I'll call home," said Susie, "and see if anything funny's happening there." When she dialled, a din of hunting horns blared from the phone.

"Turn that row down!" growled the driver.

Susie punched the 'off' button and scowled. "Aliens!" she grumbled.

"Look, I've tried to tell you, they're not aliens,"

said Greg. "Loki and the rest are ancient Norse gods."

"They come from some other world and they have technology that lets them do all kinds of amazing stuff," Susie insisted. "In my book that spells *aliens*."

When they got to the station the bus pulled into its stance and the driver slumped back in his seat with a gasp of relief. Shouldering their daypacks, Susie and Greg immediately jumped up and made for the door. When it opened, an angry supervisor climbed aboard, blocking their way.

"What's going on here, Dougie?" he demanded. "You should be well on your way to Dundee."

The driver pulled out a handkerchief to wipe the sweat from his brow. "We had to turn back," he said. "There was a... a... blockage on the road."

"There were trees in the road," an old man called out. "Trees! It's a total disgrace."

"Trees?" echoed the supervisor, screwing up his face in disbelief.

"That's right," chimed a silver-haired lady in a green coat. Greg recognised her as Mrs Gillespie, a retired teacher from his primary school. "I've an appointment with my reflexologist in Dundee, and if I'm late I'll expect the bus company to pay compensation."

"I don't think anybody's going to Dundee today," Greg muttered under his breath.

He and Susie worked their way around the supervisor and got off the bus.

"Your tickets are still valid for the whole day," the supervisor called after them.

Greg and Susie looked anxiously about them, but there were no unexpected trees or wild animals to be seen. A couple of buses were parked at the stances, their engines idling, and there were people in the waiting room staring at timetables and reading magazines.

"It all looks normal," said Susie. "What do you suppose is going on?"

"More of Loki's capers," said Greg. "He escaped Odin's exile once before, so it wouldn't surprise me if he's done it again. But plonking a wood on the edge of town seems weird even for him."

A bus marked 'Leven' pulled into the station. There was a big fuss among the passengers and the driver's face was a mixture of annoyance and astonishment.

"I'll bet you a million pounds that road is blocked as well," said Susie as they headed towards the street.

"The whole of St Andrews must be completely cut off," said Greg.

"We should head into town and have a nose about," said Susie.

When they reached the pedestrian crossing the traffic lights were blazing wildly, and not just the usual colours. They were flashing purple, orange and silver, as well as red, amber and green. Some cars had stopped, the drivers puzzling over whether they were allowed to carry on or not.

"Come on, let's nip across," said Susie, leading Greg to the other side.

They rounded the corner of Hope Park Church onto Market Street where some students were drinking coffee outside the Sombrero Café.

"Well, no trolls or goblins so far," said Greg. "That's something at least."

"It doesn't feel right, though," said Susie. She pointed to the sky. "Look at the clouds. "Don't they look funny to you?"

Greg squinted up. "Yes, they're kind of gold coloured."

They carried on down the street until they were halted by an outcry up ahead. A huge deer was charging at full speed towards them, scattering pedestrians out of its way. The great stag was as wild as the north wind, its proud head crowned with a magnificent set of antlers. There were flecks of gold in its thick brown fur and its eyes flashed a bright emerald green.

As it hurtled up Market Street people leapt aside and jumped into shop doorways. Greg and Susie pressed themselves flat against the door of a stationary shop as the stag thundered by, its hooves clattering on the pavement like an angry drumbeat.

Suddenly it pulled up and turned to face the window of a knitwear shop. In the centre of the window display, surrounded by jumpers, socks and bobble hats, was a copy of a famous painting of a stag called *The Monarch of the Glen*.

The real beast stared at it, gave a furious snort, then lowered its antlers and crashed them through the window. As glass tinkled to the ground, the stag fixed the painting with a hard stare, as if challenging a rival. It sniffed a few times then, satisfied it had cowed its opponent, took off again, galloping down the road towards Kinburn Park.

"That beastie must have come out of the forest just like the wild boar," said Susie.

"I think he's as confused as we are," said Greg. "Come on, we need to find Lewis before he gets eaten by a bear or something."

All around them the stag had left a buzz of excitement in its wake. A woman in a big hat was saying, "Somebody should phone the RSPCA."

At that moment a shadow passed across the sun. Susie glanced up and clutched Greg's arm. "Look!"

"Is that a bird?" Greg exclaimed.

The creature was gigantic, swooping in from the

south with its wings spread wide. Its scarlet and amber feathers made it seem like it was on fire.

"Look at the size of it!" Susie gasped. "It must be as big as a fighter jet."

The fiery bird sailed closer. Skimming the roof of the Victory Memorial Hall, it gave a harsh caw and pointed its sharp beak directly down Market Street.

"It's coming this way," said Susie.

Greg yanked her into the doorway of the Briteco supermarket as the crimson bird shot up the street at rooftop height. The people below instinctively ducked as it whooshed over them.

"It looks like a hawk to me," Susie muttered. "In the past people used them for hunting."

"Yes, but what is this one hunting?" Greg wondered.

At the far end of the street the bird banked and circled the roof of The Crispy Cod chip shop. Then it let out another screech and started back towards Greg and Susie. They retreated and the supermarket doors opened automatically behind them.

"I don't like the look of this," said Greg as they took shelter inside.

They crouched among the stacks of plastic baskets and watched the people in the street dashing about in panic as the giant bird dived lower.

There was a hubbub inside the store as well.

"I'm sorry," one of the checkout girls was saying to a customer, "but according to my screen you owe..." She peered at the figures on the till, "...twelve gold pieces."

Another customer was waving a receipt in the manager's face. "It says here," he declared indignantly, "I've bought two goats and a barrel of ale."

"Things are getting crazier by the minute," said Susie. "I think some kind of alien energy field is at work here. It's disrupting communications and stuff like that."

"An alien energy field?" Greg repeated. "Spinny, where do you get these random ideas from?"

"Oh, I suppose you're going to tell me it's a magic spell," said Susie. "Yes, that's very sensible!"

Greg poked his head out the door and checked both ways down the street. "At least it looks like the hawk's gone for now," he said. "Let's go."

They stepped outside and stared upward, but the sky was empty except for the gold-tinged clouds.

"We need to find Lewis in a hurry," said Susie.

Turning a deaf ear to the lingering excitement in the street, they headed for the harbour.

# 4. Not in Kansas

The police car rolled to a stop a short way from Lewis and Dave the Lobster. Two young police offers got out and paused to confer.

"When somebody phoned in about a Viking ship," said the policeman, "I thought it was a prank. But just look at this, Iona."

"Never mind how strange it is, Kenny," said the policewoman, "just play it by the book."

They walked up to Loki and glanced warily at the wolflings. "Excuse me, sir," said policeman Kenny, "but can I ask what is going on here?"

"You can ask," said Loki with a smirk, "but I don't think you would understand. It's a bit too cosmic for your puny human brain." He twirled a finger in the air to illustrate just how cosmic it all was.

"Maybe we should call Stephen Hawking," Dave the Lobster suggested. "I'll bet he could figure it out."

"Officers, maybe you should let me explain," said Lewis.

"You'd best keep out of the way, son," said Kenny.

"You too, sir," he advised Dave the Lobster.

"No problem, inspector," said Dave.

Iona the policewoman looked Loki boldly in the eye. "Do you have a licence for these creatures?" she demanded, pointing at the wolflings.

Loki squinted at her. "What?"

"You can't import wild animals into Scotland without a licence," she informed him stiffly.

"I've got news for you, chief," Loki responded with a smirk. "You're not in Scotland any more."

Iona and Kenny exchanged glances.

"I'm afraid you're a little confused, sir," said Kenny. "This is St Andrews, which is in Fife, which is in Scotland."

Loki shook his head. "We are not in Fife, we are not in Scotland, and we are definitely not in Kansas."

"Kansas, Logan?" said Dave the Lobster. "I think you've got your atlas a little mixed up."

"It's a line from *The Wizard of Oz*, you dumb cluck," Loki growled at him. He glanced at Lewis. "You know, I always thought your brother was a pain in the rump, but this guy..." With a jab of his thumb he motioned two of his wolf guards forward. "Toss him in the drink," he commanded. "That should shut him up."

Dave took a startled step back as the creatures advanced on him. "Hey, let's be cool," he pleaded with a weak smile.

The policewoman moved between them and raised a hand, causing the wolflings to pull up short.

"Get on the radio, Kenny," she said, "and call for backup."

The policeman ducked into the car and seized a radio from the dashboard.

"Look, sister, let's just be clear about this," said Loki with a sweep of his arm. "This whole town and everything in it belongs to me now."

Lewis saw Iona take a deep breath. "Whatever it is you think you're up to, sir, you're just getting yourself into trouble."

"Trouble?" Loki exclaimed. "Trouble? You don't get it, dollface. I invented trouble!"

Kenny got out of the car and joined Iona. Shaking his head, he reported, "Nothing on the radio but a lot of squeals and screeches."

"Why don't you two make yourselves scarce," said Loki. "I need to go find myself a palace."

"Actually, sir, I'll have to ask you to remain here," said Iona.

At that moment there was a gasp from the onlookers scattered about the harbour. They were all pointing upward.

A gigantic bird had appeared in the sky. It had blazing red feathers and a wingspan as wide as a goal mouth. With an ear-splitting screech it plunged down. Squawking in panic, the gulls on the harbour wall scattered in terror.

The winged predator landed with a thump on the roof of the police car, its talons scoring deep grooves in the paintwork.

"This is my pal Falkior," said Loki. "Impressive, eh?"

"It's damaging police property!" said Kenny.

The great hawk let out another piercing screech and Loki nodded, as though it were delivering a message. At a signal from the god of mischief it took off again and flew out of sight.

"I don't understand how you can even be here, Loki," said Lewis. "Odin told us he'd tossed you into some great cosmic pit of nothingness."

Loki grinned. "It's called the Ginnungagap, The Great Nothingness That Existed Before Anything Was."

"How could you possibly get out of that?" Lewis asked.

"Well, the great pit wasn't as empty as old Odin supposed, so I had a bit of help making my escape. I also came back with enough magical power to grab your town and dump it in the middle of Vanaheim."

"Vanaheim?" said Lewis. "You mean the land of the gods?"

"That's right," said Loki. "Plonked it down on top of Asgard and knocked those snotty gods and their city out of their world."

"Sir, I'm afraid you're making absolutely no sense at all," said Iona.

"If you ask me," muttered Kenny, "he's cracked in the head."

Loki grunted irritably. "Let me see if I can put it in terms you mortal flea-brains might be able to grasp," he said. "Think of Vanaheim as a billiard table and Asgard as a red ball sitting on that billiard table. This town of yours is the white ball, which I have smashed into that red ball and knocked it into a corner pocket of the table. See?"

"But where has Asgard disappeared to then?" Lewis asked. If the other gods were truly gone, he couldn't think of any way that Loki could be stopped.

Loki shrugged. "Best guess – the whole city has been knocked down into Niflheim, the land of the dead. And from there, there is *definitely* no way back."

"Wow, Elvis, you two are coming out with some cosmic stuff," said Dave. "It sounds like something out of a comic book."

"I wish it was just a comic, Dave," Lewis sighed.

The fishermen had left their boats and formed a belligerent gang. "Officers," one of them said to Kenny and Iona, "if you need any help sorting out these troublemakers, you can count on us."

The fishermen were a burly crew, but Lewis was sure they would be no match for the armed wolflings. Growling, the ferocious guards now drew their swords out of their sheaths, which made an ugly rasping sound.

"Hold it, boys," said Loki, raising a hand to restrain them. "This could get messy."

The wolflings lowered their weapons but glowered menacingly at the fishermen and the police.

"Dealing with a whole town of numbskull mortals is going to be a big headache," Loki continued. "There's another way."

He reached into his pocket and pulled out a sliver of crystal about the size of a pencil. Light gleamed inside it, matching the wicked glint in Loki's eye.

Kenny glanced at the crystal suspiciously. "That could be regarded as an offensive weapon, sir," he advised.

"Offensive?" Loki repeated mockingly. "You don't know the half of it."

As he spoke the light in the crystal grew brighter.

"Hey, look at the mist!" Dave exclaimed.

Lewis looked out over the water and saw that the great mass of mist was now sparkling with an unearthly light and rolling swiftly towards them, as though drawn to the crystal. The first billow of glittering vapour engulfed the fishermen, who immediately froze on the spot.

"Hey, what have you done to them?" Iona demanded.

She was just reaching for the truncheon on her belt when the mist reached the two officers, who instantly became as still as statues, their faces fixed in an expression of stunned surprise.

Puzzled, Dave moved towards them for a closer look.

Lewis grabbed the back of his t-shirt and restrained him. "No, Dave, we have to get away from the mist!" He released his grip and started uphill towards town.

"Yeah, I think you're right, Elvis," Dave agreed.

But before he could move, one of the wolflings seized him by his spiky hair and hauled him into the mist.

Another wolfling started after Lewis, who, spinning about, kicked a pile of lobster creels into the path of his pursuer. The wolfling's feet got tangled in the baskets and he fell flat on his muzzle.

Lewis scrambled up the path to where the walls of the ruined cathedral loomed over him. Behind him the onlookers, who hadn't moved quickly enough to escape the mist, were frozen like statues.

Lewis could feel the mist closing in on him fast. Looking around desperately for a means of escape, he spotted a bicycle lying on the grass below the cathedral wall. He heaved it upright and jumped on as the mist billowed towards him.

He pushed off and pedalled furiously towards town. Swerving round the front of the cathedral, he swept past the war memorial while the rolling mist chased after him like a hungry beast.

# 5. THE RUNAWAY MIST

As Greg and Susie headed up Market Street they passed several people shaking their mobile phones, trying to make them work. A young man raged futilely at a cash machine that was flashing the words 'Magic Beans Only' at him.

As they turned the corner into Union Street, they passed two cars that had come together nose to nose, with both drivers cursing their malfunctioning satnavs.

"Everything's going completely loopy," Susie commented.

"That's a sure sign Loki's behind it," said Greg.

They turned right into North Street past the old Salvation Army Hall. Looking down towards the cathedral they saw people hurrying up from the harbour. Among them was Tommy Wright, one of Greg's classmates. He would have run right past them if Greg hadn't grabbed his arm.

"Hang on, Tommy, where's the fire?" Greg asked.

Tommy gave him a wild-eyed look. "M-m-m-monsters down at the harbour," he stammered. "Like something out of a computer game. And the mist! It's freezing folk!" He pulled loose of Greg's grasp and ran off like he was being chased by a lion.

"Did you see Lewis there?" Susie called after him, but Tommy didn't stop to answer.

Even as she spoke, on the other side of the road, a sparkling grey mist rolled over the Younger Hall, enveloping its columns and windows. A man stepped out of the door into the mist and froze in his tracks.

"Uh-oh! This is serious!" said Susie.

"Don't just stand there, Spinny!" Greg exclaimed. "It's coming right for us!"

They spun round and ran back the way they'd come. Glancing over his shoulder, Greg saw the mist rising up to the rooftops as it poured down Union Street. Anyone caught in its path was instantly paralysed.

Greg and Susie ducked down Logie's Lane as the mist filled Market Street behind them.

"It's gaining on us!" cried Susie as they emerged into Church Square in front of the town library.

"We need a place where it can't reach us," said Greg.

The sound of ethereal voices drew their attention to Holy Trinity Church, which formed one side of the square, its spire soaring above them. Pinned to the side door facing them was a poster advertising a Norwegian choir who would be performing there that night.

"Look," said Greg, grabbing Susie by the arm, "we'll duck in here and claim sanctuary or whatever they call it."

"Greg, I don't think..." Susie began, but Greg was already dragging her inside.

He slammed the door behind them and backed away. At the far end of the church a large man in a suit was conducting the choir, who all stared at the intruders but kept on singing.

Mr Gillies the minister came rushing up to them, looking very vexed. "I'm happy for you to sit and listen to the choir," he said testily, "but we simply can't have a lot of banging and noise."

They recognised Mr Gillies from the times he'd addressed the school assembly.

"Sorry, Reverend," said Greg, "but we have to shut it out."

"It?" the minister repeated in a baffled voice. "It... out?"

"The mist," Susie explained. "It's spreading over the whole town."

The minister folded his arms and tried to look ominous. "If this is your idea of a prank," he said, "I am not amused."

"It's no prank," said Susie, pointing. "Look!"

Mist was seeping around the edges of the door and spreading over the wall. It swelled into a cloud and expanded towards them.

Greg spat out a word that was not appropriate for church as he and Susie dashed up the aisle.

Mr Gillies had just started to shout after them when the mist wrapped itself around him. He froze, with his mouth gaping open.

The mist flooded the church to their right, forcing Greg and Susie to veer left. They darted for a door just behind the choir. The singers fell silent as the cloud rolled towards them and the conductor just had time to cry out in Norwegian before they were engulfed.

"He's probably complaining about the Scottish weather," said Greg as he and Susie bashed through the door and into the passage beyond.

The passage turned a corner to the right. Racing down it, they barged through another door into a storeroom full of stacked chairs and shelves crammed with hymn books.

"This is a dead end!" Greg groaned as he shut the door on the mist, which was rolling down the corridor after them.

"No, it's not," said Susie, leaping up onto a stack of chairs. "There's a window up here."

She threw open the high window and clambered out, dropping to the other side. She landed on her feet, nimble as a cat, on the front lawn. Greg scrambled after her and flopped down on the grass.

"Come on," said Susie, helping him up.

The lawn was enclosed by a low iron railing. They swung over it easily and landed in South Street. Behind them the mist swirled around the walls of Holy Trinity and snaked its way up the spire.

"The only place safe from that stuff would be a sealed bank vault," said Greg.

"I don't think any bank is going to let you just walk into their vault," said Susie.

"Don't be so sure," said Greg. "A few words from *The Verbal Ninja* might persuade them."

"No time for that, Greg," Susie replied. "We'd better keep running."

They pelted across the street, heading for Queen's Gardens. At this point they weren't the only ones running. A sense of alarm had finally spread through the entire town and crowds of people were now trying desperately to flee the mist.

Skirting the town hall, they raced down Queen's Gardens to Queen's Terrace. From here a steep, narrow brae led down to the Kinnessburn, the stream that separated the old town from the new.

"If we can get to the bridge across the burn," Greg gasped, "maybe this stuff won't cross the water."

"I hate to say this, Greg," said Susie, "but it did come in off the sea."

They started down the brae with the mist pressing close. Susie could feel the icy touch of it on the back of her neck.

"Faster!" Greg urged.

Then he gave a strangled cry as his foot snagged on a crooked piece of paving. Susie collided with him as he pitched forward. The next instant they both tumbled head over heels down the brae, ending up in an ungainly heap at the bottom.

Before they could scramble to their feet they were completely engulfed in the mist's frigid embrace.

# 6. Evil Cat

Susie squeezed her eyes tight shut, expecting something like an electric shock as the mist took its paralysing effect. Instead all she felt was a slight chill. When she opened her eyes she saw Greg grinning at her.

"Hey, we're okay!" he exclaimed.

"Yes, why is that?" said Susie.

"Maybe we're just tougher than everybody else," Greg suggested.

"No, I don't think so," said Susie, staring at her Asgardian ring. "It must be these."

Greg gazed at his ring too. "Becauuse Odin gave them to us?"

"They must have some kind of power that's protecting us," said Susie.

"Well, that's a relief," said Greg. "I didn't fancy spending the rest of my life as a statue in somebody's museum."

"Take it from me, Greg," said Susie with a chuckle, "nobody would consider you a work of art."

They picked themselves up and looked around. The mist was so thick, they could barely see more than an arm's length ahead.

"Do you think Lewis got away from the harbour in time?" Susie wondered.

"If he did get away, I expect he headed for home," said Greg.

"That's where we're off to then," said Susie.

A few steps brought them onto the bridge over the Kinnessburn. They could hear the faint trickle of the stream as they crossed over and turned right along Kinnessburn Road.

"Hang on a second," said Greg in an urgent whisper. "There's somebody following us."

"You're right," Susie agreed. She could hear what sounded like footfalls behind them.

Suddenly there came a harsh cackling noise.

They spun round to confront their pursuer. Susie braced herself, ready to fight off something with three heads. Instead, a pair of ducks waddled past, still quacking at each other, totally unconcerned with the two humans.

Susie heaved a sigh of relief.

"It must be bad when we get spooked by Donald Duck," said Greg.

"That stuff must not affect animals," said Susie. "And look, the sun's breaking through."

The mist was thinning and in a matter of seconds the air cleared completely.

"Well, that's a bonus," said Greg. "Now we can put on a bit of speed."

They jogged past the bowling club and up Pipeland Road, passing various people frozen in mid-stride or seated inside their stalled cars. A flock of sparrows flitted across the sky, further proof that only humans had been affected.

"We're probably the only people in St Andrews who can still move," said Greg.

They were headed along Lamond Drive when they heard a dreadful screech. It was the cry of the fiery hawk, which came swooping over the nearby rooftops.

"Freeze!" said Greg.

He and Susie stopped dead in their tracks, doing their best to look as if they had been paralysed like everybody else. They held their breath, not daring to move a muscle as the shadow of the bird of prey passed over them. They held their poses stiffly until the creature disappeared from view.

"I think it's gone," said Greg.

Susie relaxed and gave herself a shake. "I never thought pretending to be a tree in drama class would ever come in so handy."

Hurrying along, they finally reached Bannock Street,

where the McBride family lived.

"It's just as well Mum and Dad are in Dunfermline for the day, visiting Aunt Vivian," said Greg.

"What, that horrible aunt of yours that nobody likes?"

"Dad calls it a pre-emptive strike," said Greg, "to keep her from visiting us and staying for a week."

They were walking up the street when a large dog came racing past them, howling in terror. It belonged to their neighbours, the Larkins, and it was in serious trouble.

Chasing after it, spitting and hissing, was a large ginger cat. This cat had been in so many fights it had lost tufts of fur from all over its body, and it only had one ear, which made it look even fiercer.

"Mrs Mulheron's cat!" said Greg as he and Susie dodged aside.

The two pets flew past, the cat slashing with its front claws and narrowly missing the dog's tail.

"I hate that wee monster!" Susie exclaimed as the animals disappeared round the corner into Learmonth place.

"I can't believe Mrs Mulheron calls it Tiddles," said Greg. "It should be called Fangface or Terrorclaw or something like that."

"My mum calls it Evil Cat," said Susie. "It terrorises every pet in the neighbourhood."

"And a lot of the people too," said Greg. "It should be declared a public enemy."

In the distance they heard a savage squall from the cat as it pursued the hapless dog around the block.

Outside the McBride house a discarded bicycle lay on its side on the pavement. Halfway up the front path they saw Lewis. He was frozen in mid-step as he made a mad dash for the front door.

They hurried over to him and Susie stared into his lifeless eyes. "Oh, no, the mist got him!"

"The mug!" Greg exclaimed in disgust. "I told him to wear his ring, but oh no, he was scared it would turn him into a toadstool or something."

"If we can find his ring and stick it on his finger, maybe that will snap him out of it," said Susie.

"Maybe," Greg agreed. "But we can't leave him standing around outside with Loki's overgrown budgie out looking for us."

"You grab his legs then," said Susie, "and I'll take his arms."

Lewis was as rigid as a plank and his body didn't change position at all as they carried him into the front room and laid him down on the sofa.

"Look at the state of him!" said Greg, shaking his head. "It's as if he's trying to run up to the ceiling."

"Never mind how he looks," said Susie. "Where does he keep his ring?"

"Probably in his room some place," said Greg. He led the way upstairs. "He told me he could grab it quickly if he ever needed it."

"I just hope we can find it," said Susie.

"Don't worry, it'll be a cinch," Greg assured her as they entered the room. "He keeps this place as tidy as an operating theatre."

A glance around Lewis' room showed Susie that Greg hadn't exaggerated. The books in the three large bookcases were organised into fiction and non-fiction and arranged alphabetically. The bed was neatly made and everything on the desk was sensibly arranged, sheets of paper and magazines carefully stacked, pens and pencils gathered in cups by colour.

"Is he expecting the Queen to drop by or something?" Susie wondered.

"No, he's just nuts, if you ask me," Greg replied.

A large glass tank near the foot of the bed was home to two goldfish. At the bottom of the tank were various pebbles and pieces of crystal as well as a plastic castle around which the fish occasionally swam.

"These fish are really cute," said Susie.

"He calls them Ishmael and Ahab," said Greg. "Heaven only knows why."

He went to work on the drawers, tossing socks, jumpers and underwear in all directions. Susie meanwhile examined the desk and its contents. By the time she finished Greg was hauling the covers off Lewis' bed and heaving the pillows aside.

"This is ridiculous," he grunted. "You'd think he'd made it invisible."

Suddenly Susie's attention was caught by a ragged orange shape at the foot of the bed, staring hungrily into the fish tank. It had one claw raised, ready to plunge in and snatch one of the goldfish.

"Evil Cat!" she yelled and rushed to shoo it off.

The cat recoiled, pressing itself against the wall and hissing. It bared its yellow teeth and raked the air with its claws.

"Get out of here!" Greg bellowed, plucking a pillow from the floor and flinging it at the animal.

The cat dodged aside, dropped to the floor, and dashed out the door with an angry snarl.

"It must have got in through an open window," said Greg. "Really, we should get the police on to that monster."

"There, there, Ishmael," Susie soothed the goldfish. "Don't you worry, Ahab. That horrid cat's gone." She peered more closely into the water and said, "What's all this stuff at the bottom?"

"He puts all kinds of random junk in there," said Greg. "He says it provides them with stimulation.

Why anybody wants to stimulate a fish is beyond me."

"There's all sorts of stuff down there," said Susie. "Rocks, pebbles, crystals—"

"And a stupid plastic castle," said Greg. "So what?"

"I can see a glint of gold," replied Susie.

"Right, let's have it then," said Greg, peering into the water and rolling up his sleeve.

He hesitated with his hand hovering over the water. "You know, I'm sure those fish don't like me. Look at the way Ahab is glowering at me."

"Don't be silly, Greg," said Susie, plunging her arm in. "They won't bite." Raking through the sand at the bottom, she uncovered a golden ring, pinched it between her thumb and forefinger and lifted it out.

"Bingo!" said Greg, plucking it from her grasp. "Let's go put it on him."

They trooped downstairs, where Lewis was still flat on his back on the sofa, his limbs frozen in a running motion.

"He *would* have his hands in a really awkward position," Greg complained, tilting Lewis' motionless form towards him to get a better angle.

"I hope this works," said Susie.

Greg forced the ring onto the third finger of Lewis' right hand then stepped back. He and Susie watched anxiously, waiting for something to happen.

"I thought there'd be a flash of light or something," said Greg.

"Give it time," said Susie. "Maybe it takes a minute or two to take effect – you know, like aspirin."

Just then Lewis made a choking sound and rolled off the sofa onto the floor. Seeing Susie and Greg, he croaked, "Big trouble – Loki's back!"

"We sort of guessed that," said Greg, helping him up.

"Have you seen him?" asked Susie.

Lewis nodded. "Down at the harbour. I was running to the house to get my ring. I had a notion it might protect me."

"We had the same idea," said Susie, "so we found it and stuck it on your finger. How do you feel?"

"A bit dizzy," said Lewis, "but I think I'm okay. What are you two doing here? I thought you went to Dundee."

"The bus got stopped by a forest," said Greg.

"And a wild boar the size of a Mini," Susie added.

Suddenly all three of their rings began to glow brightly and the TV switched itself on. The screen was a mass of static and it gave off a distorted noise that might or might not be a voice.

"The TV's messed up like everything else," said Greg, looking round for the remote control. "We might as well switch it off."

"No, wait," said Susie. "Look!"

The static cleared and in its place was the face of a man wearing a gold helmet. He had a long white beard and a black patch over his right eye.

"It's just some old guy with a beard and an eyepatch," Greg snorted. "It must be a pirate film."

"Don't you recognise him?" said Lewis. "That's Odin, king of the gods."

# 7. FRIGHT AT THE MUSEUM

Odin raised a hand in greeting. His voice was broken and distorted and was not in sync with the movement of his lips, but they were able to make out a few words amidst the interference.

"BRZZZT... LOKI... URRRZZZZZ... STAFF... ZZZZZEEE... OUNT... DAGGER... URRZZZZZ... BLEEEEEE... PROTECT... OOZZEEEE... ASGARD... RRZZZZZ..."

Static flooded the screen once more and a piercing electronic whine filled the air. Flashing zigzags grew brighter as the noise grew louder. The TV began to shake violently.

"Take cover!" Greg yelled. All three of them dived behind the sofa.

The next instant the television screen exploded all over the carpet, leaving an empty frame behind.

Greg poked his head up and groaned, "We've only had that set a few weeks."

"The alien energy must have overloaded it," said Susie

as they emerged from cover.

"The rings have stopped glowing," Lewis observed.

"Now we know why Odin gave them to us," said Susie. "It was so he could contact us in a crisis."

"Not that he told us much," grumbled Greg. "It was mostly buzzing and crackling."

Susie turned to Lewis. "Maybe you should tell us what happened at the harbour."

"Let's do it in the kitchen while I whip up some sandwiches," Greg suggested.

"Ace idea!" said Susie. "I'm starved."

Once they were seated round the kitchen table with cans of cola and a pile of ham and cheese sandwiches, Lewis gave them a brief account of Loki's arrival by longship, his wolfling guards, and how he summoned the mist. Greg and Susie told him about their interrupted bus journey and all the strange things they had experienced since.

"So St Andrews is going weird because it's been teleported to the land of Vanaheim, the land of the Norse gods," said Susie, polishing off her last bite of sandwich.

"That explains the forest and the colour of the sea," said Greg. He paused to drain his can of cola. "But what about the traffic lights, the cash machine and the rest?"

Lewis thought about that. "Normally they would be part of the national power grid, but obviously they can't be attached to that now because we're in a different world."

"Since we're in Vanaheim," mused Susie, "all that stuff must be plugged into a field of cosmic energy that provides power for this place."

"Can't we just say it's magic?" said Greg.

"*A field of cosmic energy*," Susie insisted. She pointed at the last sandwich Lewis had left on his plate untouched. "Are you going to eat that or what?"

"Help yourself," said Lewis.

Susie grabbed the sandwich and took a big bite.

"Well, whatever you call this energy field," said Lewis, "Odin used it to send us a message. But what was he trying to tell us?"

"It's pretty clear he wants us to protect Asgard," said Susie through a mouthful of sandwich.

"How are we supposed to do that?" wondered Greg. "From what you say, Lewis, Asgard's been blasted away to the land of the dead!"

"That's what Loki told me," said Lewis.

"He could be wrong about that," said Susie, "or he could be lying just to fool us."

"Well, wherever Asgard is, we're going to need a dagger to defend it," said Greg. "Odin definitely said we need a dagger."

"A dagger? I have to tell you, I don't have one on me," said Susie.

"Do you think a kitchen knife would do?" Lewis suggested.

"If Odin had meant a kitchen knife, I'm pretty sure he would have said a kitchen knife," Greg informed him.

"Dagger it is then," said Susie, taking a swig of cola. "So where are we going to get one of those? You won't find one in the supermarket."

Lewis frowned for a moment. "The museum's got a Viking exhibition going on just now. Maybe there's a dagger on display there."

"A Viking dagger? That would be just the thing," said Greg cheerfully.

"Then what?" asked Susie. "How do we protect Asgard when we don't know where it is?"

"Maybe Odin will send another message once we have the dagger," said Lewis.

"Then we'd better not hang about," said Greg. He stood up and brushed the crumbs off the front of his jumper. "Let's get to the museum. Where is it?"

"It's in Kinburn Park," said Lewis. "Have you never been there?"

"They made us go in primary school once," said Greg. "All I remember is eating crisps in the tearoom."

They left the kitchen and headed down the hallway to the front door.

"Once we get our hands on that dagger, the rest will be a piece of cake," Greg asserted confidently as he flung open the door.

Two snarling wolflings loomed on the doorstep, swords in hand.

Greg slammed the door in their faces and turned to the others. "Maybe it won't be so easy."

The door shuddered under a heavy blow and the three of them recoiled. There came a crash from the rear of the house.

"They're coming in through the back as well!" Susie cried.

The front door bashed open and the wolflings bounded inside with a feral gleam in their eyes.

"This way!" yelled Greg and they all dived into the front room.

Growling deep in their throats, the wolflings followed their prey. Two more came barging in from the kitchen, fangs gleaming hungrily.

Lewis glanced right and left. "We're trapped!" he groaned.

"You prisoners now," one of the wolflings rumbled.

"I don't know about you two," said Susie, "but I'm not giving in without a fight."

"A fight?" Lewis echoed incredulously. "There are four of them and they all have swords and very pointy teeth!"

"They're not so tough, Lewis," said Greg. "I bet we can take them." He snatched a cushion off the sofa and got ready to throw it. Susie grabbed hold of a table lamp and brandished it like a club.

The wolflings closed in. Just then a savage "SCREEOWR!" from behind halted them in their tracks. Neck fur bristling, they turned to see who was bold enough to challenge them.

There in the hall doorway, swelling itself up to its largest size, its eyes blazing with malice, stood Evil Cat. Far from being afraid of the wolflings, it looked eager to take them on.

The effect on the wolflings was electrifying. They turned on the cat as one, their yellow eyes flashing, savage growls vibrating in their throats.

Evil Cat spat defiance at them.

Prisoners forgotten, the wolflings lunged at their new enemy. With a malevolent hiss Evil Cat turned and fled. The wolflings instinctively gave chase, slashing at the air with their swords. In a pack they pursued Evil Cat out the back door.

"Wow!" said Greg. "You'd think Loki would have them better trained."

"We'd better get out of here before the cat shakes them off and they remember what they came for," said Susie.

The three of them ran out the front door and

down Bannock Street. In the distance they could hear the wolflings' howls as they hunted Evil Cat along Lindsay Gardens.

"Right," said Greg, "which way to Kinburn Park?"

"We should keep under cover," Susie advised, "in case that giant hawk's out looking for us."

"Let's take the Lade Braes Walk," suggested Lewis. "There are plenty of trees there to hide us."

They hurried down to the Lade Braes and followed the path that ran beside the burn. Tall oaks and beech trees shaded the whole route with their spreading branches. From there they turned up onto Doubledykes Road.

All along the way they passed people paralysed mid-step, which Lewis found unsettling. "It's like walking through a huge waxworks," he murmured.

"I just hope everybody will wake up again," said Susie.

"No worries, Spinny," said Greg, clapping her on the shoulder. "We woke Lewis up and he's right as rain. Aren't you, Lewis?"

"I guess so," said Lewis. "Although, now that you mention it, my stomach's a bit queasy. I think the cheese in those sandwiches was a bit off."

"Never mind your stomach!" said Greg. "Here's the park now."

They entered Kinburn Park and followed a paved

drive up to the museum. From the outside it looked like a miniature castle. A sign by the door advertised teas and coffees in the café.

All the lights inside were flickering an eerie green colour. At the reception desk sat a Goth girl in pink glasses, one hand stretched out towards the telephone. Beyond her was the café where several customers were seated, some with cups in their hands, one with a piece of cake on its way into his mouth. The flickering light made the motionless figures look like zombies, just waiting to lurch into unnatural life.

"I wish the lights would stop doing that," said Susie with a shudder.

"Come on, it's not like the place is haunted," said Greg.

An opening to their right led to a room where items from the history of St Andrews were on display. There were photographs of Market Street in Victorian times, a wartime gas mask, a sign from a cinema that shut down in the 1970s, and even some railway timetables from when trains stopped at the town. On the far wall was a screen that usually showed old newsreels.

"The Viking exhibit is upstairs," said Lewis.

"No, come and look at this," said Susie, beckoning them over to the screen.

On the screen they saw a lofty mountain with mysterious silver clouds swirling about its craggy summit. As if issuing from the mountain itself, they heard the voice of Odin. Lewis felt the ring on his finger begin to tingle as they pressed in closer to hear. All three of them strained their ears, trying to distinguish Odin's words from the static interference.

"RRRZZ ZZZ... FLASH... BZZZT... RESCUE... URRRZZZ... GURDA..."

The screen flickered and the face of Odin, one-eyed and white-bearded, superimposed itself upon the mountain.

"SKKKRRK... STAFF... ZZZEEE... THREE... DZIZIZ..."

There was a dazzling flash and the picture reverted to some horse-drawn wagons moving over a cobbled marketplace.

"It's gone back to its usual film," said Lewis.

"Well, that little message was about as much help as a Chinese crossword puzzle," said Greg.

"But he's definitely trying to tell us something. Come on, we'd best get upstairs and look for that dagger," said Susie.

They climbed up to the first floor. The atmosphere here was even more unsettling. The strange light played over a Viking helmet on loan from a museum in Orkney, and made the dragon eyes on a model longship glint as if they were alive. There were some glass cases displaying old coins and ancient jewellery. Beyond them stood a dummy dressed in a monk's hooded robe, recalling the days when the monks had to barricade their monasteries against Viking raiders.

"I don't see any dagger," said Lewis, disappointed.

"Me neither," said Susie. "Let's get out of here. This place is too spooky."

"Do you think there are ghosts hiding in the shadows?" asked Greg with a grin. "Maybe we should call Scooby Doo."

"Greg, don't joke about ghosts," said Susie.

They turned back towards the stairs, and as they did, the hooded monk lurched into motion and staggered towards them.

"Run!" Susie cried. "The place *is* haunted!"

# 8. Everything Is Under Control

Greg, Susie and Lewis fell back as the monk stumbled towards them like a monster from a horror film.

"Loki's brought it to life!" cried Susie.

"Run before it gets us!" said Greg.

Just as they all turned to flee, a voice called out, "Steady on, Elvis, it's only me!"

Lewis recognised the voice at once and they all stopped. When they turned around they saw the monk throw back his hood to reveal the smiling face and spiky hair of Dave the Lobster.

"Dave!" Lewis exclaimed. "But how...?"

"You know this guy, Lewis?" said Greg.

"He's Dave," said Lewis, "Dave, er..."

"Dave the Lobster," Dave interjected proudly. "Pleased to meet you."

"Dave's from the university," Lewis explained. "He gave a talk to my class."

"About lobsters," Dave added, peeling off the monk's robe to reveal his Rock Lobster t-shirt.

"Dave, this is my brother Greg," said Lewis. "And this is Susie."

They all shook hands. "What are you doing here, Dave?" Lewis wondered. "The mist paralysed everybody else."

Dave shrugged. "When the mist got to me I felt fine, but I saw what happened to the two coppers and decided to play it crafty. I stand there still as a statue so Logan and his pals will ignore me, and eventually they slope off."

"He means Loki, " Lewis whispered to Greg and Susie.

"That was quick thinking," Susie complimented Dave.

"You don't get an article published in Marine Science Monthly without having a few brains," said Dave. "By the way, it was about the migration patterns of the North Atlantic lobster."

"That doesn't explain what you're doing in the museum," said Lewis.

"Or why you were dressed up as a monk," said Greg.

"Oh, right," said Dave the Lobster. "Well, once the mist clears, I see that everyone is frozen. It looks like Logan and his pals are taking over the town, and they've all got swords. I decide I'd better arm up, and the only place I'm likely to find a sword is here, at the museum."

"It makes sense," said Susie. "I wish I had my hockey stick."

"It's too bad there aren't any swords or daggers here," grumped Greg.

"When I hear you coming," Dave resumed, "I think it might be Logan. There's no place to hide, then I bumped into this dummy monk. Right, I think, I'll have his clobber, ditch him behind that display case and take his place. So, you here looking for swords as well, eh?"

"Something like that," said Greg.

"Well, we're no further forward, are we?" Lewis complained. "What's going to happen when Mum and Dad get back from Dunfermline? Are they going to fall into a gigantic hole in the ground where St Andrews used to be?"

"Maybe there'll be some kind of dimensional barrier that nobody can get past," Susie suggested.

"Never mind about that just now," said Greg. "The point is that Loki's stolen our town and he's not getting away with it. We're on a mission from Odin and nothing is going to stop us."

"I'd feel a bit more unstoppable if I knew what the mission was," said Lewis.

"Well, the first step," said Susie, "is to find out what Loki's up to and then think of a way to trip him up."

"Good plan," said Greg. "Messing things up for Loki is what we do best."

"Look, I'm totally with you on this whole plan thing," Dave the Lobster put in, "but can somebody please explain what's going on? For a start, who is this Edwin guy you keep talking about?"

"That's *Odin*," Greg corrected him.

He was about to say more when Lewis dug him in the ribs and signalled for quiet. "There's somebody coming up the stairs," he whispered.

They all shrank back into the shadows and crouched there. Lewis could hear the stairs creaking beneath two pairs of footsteps. He held his breath as one uniformed figure wearing sunglasses appeared first, then another.

"Hello? Is anybody here?" enquired a female voice.

"It's okay, it's the police," said Lewis, heaving a sigh of relief.

Kenny and Iona stood at the top of the stairs, gazing around the room, their eyes hidden by dark glasses.

Everybody stood up and came out of hiding.

"Oh yeah, they were down at the harbour," Dave told Greg and Susie.

It did seem odd to Lewis that they should be wearing dark glasses indoors, but Dave stepped forward to greet them. "Good to see you, officers," he grinned.

"I thought you were both frozen by the mist," said Lewis.

"Don't be dim, Elvis," said Dave. "They must be immune, just like me."

"Yes, we're immune," said Kenny in a flat voice.

"We're really glad you're here," said Susie. "My cousin Gina is a police officer in Glasgow."

"Yes, she is," Iona agreed woodenly.

It worried Lewis that the two police officers didn't sound like themselves. He stared at them, trying to see their eyes, but all that showed in the dark lenses was a reflection of the room and its eerily flickering lights.

"You must come with us," Iona instructed.

"To a place of safety," Kenny added.

"What about Loki and his guard dogs?" asked Greg.

"And that giant bird?" said Lewis.

"The emergency services have taken control," said Iona.

"Yes, everything is under control," Kenny agreed. "Now follow us."

Without another word the two police officers turned and headed back down the stairs.

"Well, that's a relief," said Dave the Lobster, as he and the three youngsters followed. "I hope they've got some grub at this emergency station. I'm famished.

Did you know lobsters have two stomachs? Just think how hungry they must get."

There was a white van waiting outside the museum entrance. Kenny opened the back door and waved them inside.

"You will be safe in there," Iona assured them.

The four of them climbed inside and sat down on small benches that ran up both sides. Kenny slammed the door shut and they heard it clunk.

"Did they just lock us in?" Lewis asked.

"Relax, Lewis," said Greg. "It's probably just a safety precaution."

The two police officers climbed in the front where only the backs of their heads were visible through a tiny grille. The engine started up and the van moved up the narrow road through the park and into the street.

"Well, I'm glad all that nuttiness is over," said Dave the Lobster. "You know what? I'll bet it was just a hallucination, like the weird dreams you have when you eat too much Swiss cheese before bed."

"What's cheese got to do with it?" asked Greg.

"That's just an example," said Dave. "Probably there's been a chemical spill at sea, and the wind's blown the fumes into the town, which made our minds play tricks on us."

"Dave, it's not a hallucination," Lewis began. He wasn't

sure how well the marine biologist would get his head around the truth, but he felt he had to try. "The fact is, that guy Loki, he's a Norse god, the god of magic."

"And of being a pain in the neck," Greg added.

"He's been in St Andrews before, using his magic to cause trouble," said Lewis. "This time he's magically transported the whole town to Vanaheim, the land of the gods. That's why things have become so weird."

Dave the Lobster gave him a quizzical look. "Elvis, are you sure you're not still hallucinating?"

"Look, lobster man," Greg put in impatiently, "we've run into Loki before, and travelled to Asgard, and met Thor and..." His voice petered out as he realised Dave was staring at him like he was speaking Japanese.

"Let me explain it," said Susie. "Look, Dave, Loki is an alien using advanced technology to perform amazing feats."

"Technology," Dave repeated. "Right, I'm with you now."

"He's teleported St Andrews into an alternate dimension where the physical laws are different and evolution has followed a path that's created unusual creatures like the wolves and the giant hawk."

"Alternate dimension," said Dave, nodding. "Okay."

"Everything in this dimension is powered by a field of cosmic energy," Susie continued, "which has been causing the flickering lights and other effects."

Dave nodded knowingly and turned to Greg who was seated beside him. "Say, Gary, your girlfriend is a bit of a science whizz, eh?"

"No, she just watches a lot of science fiction," said Greg. "And by the way, she is *not* my girlfriend."

Susie stifled a snort of laughter.

Lewis peered out the small, grimy window at the back of the van trying to make out where they were going. Progress was slow as the police officers manoeuvred around all the cars that had stalled in the middle of the road when the mist rolled in.

"I've been wondering," Susie said to Dave, "why didn't the mist freeze you like everybody else?"

Dave the Lobster shrugged. "I suppose I'm just immune, like the three of you."

"We're not immune," said Greg. "We're protected by these gold rings." He extended his hand to show Dave the ring he was wearing.

Dave let out a low whistle. "Pretty flash," he said.

"But you're not wearing a ring," Lewis pointed out.

"Hmm, that's right, Elvis," said Dave. He lapsed into thought for several seconds. Then a big smile spread over his face. "I see now. I may not have one of those rings, but I've got something just as snazzy." He patted the front of his t-shirt.

"A picture of a lobster wouldn't protect you," said Susie.

"No matter how much you like them," Lewis added.

"No, no, listen," said Dave. "My girlfriend Inga, she's from Denmark, right? So when she had to go home a few months back we sort of got engaged. I gave her my lobster-claw necklace to wear and she gave me this."

He pulled out an object that was hanging by a chain around his neck. It was a piece of crystal in the shape of an upside-down 'T' with a streak of gold running through it.

"She said it belonged to her gran," Dave continued. "It's been in the family for hundreds of years."

"It looks dead old," said Susie.

Lewis peered closely. "And that bit of gold inside it looks the same as what our rings are made of – Asgardian gold."

"That's a stroke of luck, eh?" said Dave. "Asgardian? Does that mean it comes from South Africa?"

"No, Dave," said Greg. "It comes from a lot further away than that."

"That 'T' shape is the symbol of Thor, the god of thunder," said Lewis. "I'll bet he gave it as a present to one of your girlfriend's ancestors centuries ago."

"Wow! Cool!" said Dave.

"That still doesn't account for our two friends in blue," said Greg. "It's not very likely that they've got Asgardian gold on them as well."

"No, it's not as if you can pick it up at a car boot sale," said Susie.

"There's something strange about them," said Lewis. "It's like they're not the same people they were before."

"You're right," Dave chipped in. "They're kind of stiff, you know, like plastic models come to life."

"And what's this safe place they were talking about?" Greg wondered. "If we're in the middle of Vanaheim, where are we going to be safe?"

At that moment the van slowed to a halt.

"Where are we?" Greg asked.

"It's hard to see much through this mucky window," said Lewis, "but I think we're outside the town hall."

"I suppose that's an obvious place for the emergency services to set up," said Dave.

Kenny and Iona got out of the van, walked round to the back and opened the door. The four passengers clambered out and found themselves surrounded by half a dozen wolflings with their swords drawn.

"Hey, what's the game here?" Greg demanded.

The two police officers pulled off their sunglasses. Underneath, their eyes were glazed, as though they'd been hypnotised. They spoke in unison like a pair of machines: "Lord Loki has summoned you."

They pointed to the open doorway of the town hall. The wolflings prodded the prisoners with the points of their swords, driving them inside.

# 9. Interior Decoration

Inside the town hall the lights were playing the same tricks as elsewhere, shifting abruptly through every colour in the rainbow. The four prisoners were herded into a large room off to the right of the entrance hall. Lewis remembered coming here to see a display of model railways a few months ago. The room looked very different now.

Nailed to the walls, seemingly at random, were a round wooden shield, the front bumper from a sports car, a set of antlers, a motorcycle helmet and a metal sign that read 'ROAD WORKS'.

Tables and chairs had been pushed to the sides to form an aisle leading to where Loki was trying his best to look kingly. He was seated on a large wooden chair that had been carelessly daubed with gold paint. Behind him hung two threadbare Scottish flags. A symbol of two snakes biting each other's tails had been clumsily painted on the space between the flags. Lewis recognised it as Loki's personal symbol, though it was so crudely done it might have been a pair of rubber hoses chasing each other.

Off to Loki's left on a small wooden table sat a crystal the size of an Easter egg. The flickering lights reflected eerily from its polished facets.

"Logan, good to see you!" Dave the Lobster exclaimed. "I see you've done the place up a bit."

Loki frowned at the makeshift decorations, then at his wolfling guards. "I told these dumb-bells to find war trophies, a few banners or serpents' heads, to turn the place into a throne room," he grumbled, "and this is what they came up with." He squirmed uncomfortably in his chair. "Isn't there even one decent throne in this town?" he complained. Abruptly he shot to his feet, knocking the chair back against the wall. "Was this really the best you could do?" he demanded of his guards.

The wolflings' ears drooped unhappily.

"Not much for interior design, are they?" said Greg.

"No, but it seems they're really good at *chasing cats*," spat Loki accusingly.

The wolflings threw back their heads and howled miserably. Loki made a chopping motion with his hand to silence them.

"Is that why you sent the police to get us this time?" said Lewis.

"Yes, what have you done to Kenny and Iona?" Susie demanded.

Loki smirked. "I put them under my control."

"You won't find it so easy to control our minds," Greg warned him belligerently.

"Kid, a screwy mind like yours you can keep to yourself," said Loki, making a 'hands off' gesture.

"How did you know where to find us?" Susie asked.

"Those rings Odin gave you may protect you against certain kinds of enchantment," Loki answered, "but whenever they're activated, they're a dead giveaway to anybody with a sense of magic."

"Like you, you mean," said Lewis.

"Right on, shorty," Loki responded smugly.

Suddenly the lights gave off an azure flash that made them all jump.

"I really wish the lights would stop goofing around," said Loki through gritted teeth.

"You need a good electrician," said Susie. "You should call my Uncle Pete."

"I'll let you know when I want help from your Uncle Pete!" Loki snapped.

Greg casually folded his arms. "So is this the bit where you tell us how you're going to rule the whole universe?"

"There won't be any universe to rule if *he* gets his hands on it," Loki answered grimly.

"Who are you talking about?" asked Lewis.

"Kid, remember down at the harbour when we were talking over old times?" said Loki.

"Like when Odin kicked you down a deep dark hole," said Susie.

"That deep dark hole has a name, toots," said Loki. "It's called the Ginnungagap."

"Don't call me toots!" Susie warned.

"Anyway," Lewis interrupted, "you told me you weren't down that black hole alone."

"Too true," Loki confirmed. "*He* was there – Ymir."

Lewis was surprised to see him shudder.

"Who's this Emir, Logan?" asked Dave the Lobster. "A pal of yours?"

"Ymir is nobody's pal," said Loki. "He was the original ice giant, so huge he could use Mount Everest for a toothpick, so evil he could dim the sun just by looking at it."

"Are you saying he's a bigger creep than you?" said Greg.

"Kid, compared to Ymir, I'm a fluffy pink bunny dishing out lollipops and candy," said Loki. "Thousands of years ago, after an epic battle, Odin beat Ymir and pitched him down into the depths of the Ginnungagap. Everybody thought he was dead."

"You're telling us they were wrong?" said Susie.

Loki nodded. It was hard to tell in the weird light, but his face seemed to have turned pale. "You know what it's like when you're all alone in a dark room then you hear somebody breathing behind you? That's what it was like for me when I realised I wasn't the only one in the pit."

"I'm guessing this Emir wasn't interested in passing the time with a few rounds of snap," said Dave the Lobster.

"He was mad," said Loki. "Real mad. Even before he was tossed into the pit, he wasn't exactly big on laughs. But after all the millennia he's spent down there, he hates everyone and everything."

"Sounds grim," said Lewis. For the first time ever he actually felt sorry for Loki.

"Grim doesn't even come close," said Loki. "Just imagine being trapped in a pitch-black void with the most powerful, the most evil giant who ever existed. I'll be having bad dreams for a long, long time."

"If this powerful giant couldn't escape from the Ginnungagap, how did you get out?" Lewis asked.

"Ymir has lots of power, but he's big," Loki explained, "so big that he can't haul himself out of the pit without help. His first thought when he found me was that he could entertain himself by taking a really long time to kill me. Luckily I persuaded him that I had a better idea: if he helped me escape, then once I was out, I would spring him as well. After we'd made a deal with lots of oaths and stuff, he shot me out of there like firing me out of a pea-shooter."

"But you must have known Odin would find out you were back," said Susie.

"Then it would be back to happy times in the dark with your new BFF," said Greg.

"Yeah, I knew that," said Loki. "That's why I had to get rid of Odin and the rest before doing anything else. No way was I going to let them send me back there."

"Hang on," said Lewis. "Even when you had all your godly power, you could never pull off anything as big as moving the whole of St Andrews into another world."

"Ymir gave me a little gift, which I was supposed to use to haul him up out of the Ginnungagap," said Loki, indicating the crystal on the table to his left. "It's a shard from Ymir's icy heart. Down in the void it can't do anything, but out here in the real world it lets me tap into a primal magic from the beginning of the universe."

"That's the crystal you pulled out at the harbour," said Lewis, "but it's a lot bigger now."

"Yeah, it keeps growing," said Loki. He frowned at the crystal and rubbed his beard nervously. "And it's getting harder and harder to control." He wrenched his gaze away from the shard. "Anyway, instead of using it to bring Ymir back into the universe, I used it to shift your little town off the Earth and drop it in Vanaheim, knocking Asgard right out of this world."

"Why St Andrews?" Susie wondered. "Why not some place else, like Bathgate or Irvine?"

"The spell only works on a place that's already charged with magic," said Loki, "like your little town."

"Yes, because of all the enchantments you've cast here before," Lewis surmised.

"Sure," said Loki. "So now here we are in my new capital. Such as it is."

"This is just crazy," said Greg, "knocking towns and cities around like they were..."

"Billiard balls?" Loki suggested. "I hope the old gang are happy in whatever oblivion they've ended up in."

"So you're welching on your deal with Ymir?" asked Greg.

"Of course I am!" said Loki emphatically. "If that big lug ever gets loose he'll kill every living thing in the universe, starting with me."

"So what is it you want from us?" Lewis asked.

"I'm going to need a bit of help getting that shard back under control," said Loki, casting an uneasy eye over the crystal.

"You'll not get any help from us, you sleaze," Susie told him.

"All I need from you, sporty girl, is those rings you're wearing," said Loki.

Susie took up a fighting pose. "Just you try and take them."

"They were a gift from Odin to *us*," said Lewis. "If you try to use them, they'll probably blow up in your face."

"It would be just like him to pull a dirty trick like that!" Loki growled. He launched into a lengthy list of grievances against Odin that had accumulated over the past two thousand years.

While Loki was busy complaining, Greg sidled closer to Dave the Lobster. Out of the side of his mouth he said, "Right, Dave, while he's distracted, you watch my back and I'll make a grab for that rock."

"Careful there, Gary," Dave warned. "That thing looks as dangerous as a poisonous anemone."

"Thanks for the tip," said Greg. Keeping a cautious eye on the wolflings, he edged closer to the crystal. Choosing his moment, he made a dive for it.

As soon as he touched it, beams of cold blue energy blazed from the heart of the stone. Greg was hurled back as though he'd been struck down by an electric shock. As he tumbled across the floor, a golden blaze shone from his Asgardian ring.

Lewis and Susie's rings flared as well. Dave the

Lobster let out a yelp as a golden radiance lit up the amulet under his t-shirt. The wolflings scattered, yelping like startled dogs.

"Stop that yammering and grab those mortals, you stupid hounds!" yelled Loki.

Greg scrambled to his feet as the glow from the rings subsided. Still whimpering, the beast guards surrounded the four prisoners and seized them.

"Enough fooling around," said Loki, taking a step towards them. "I'll have those rings now."

Suddenly the door burst open and a woman in chain-mail armour bounded into the room, long blonde hair flying behind her like a banner. She swept her sword from its sheath and cried, "For Odin and Asgard!"

# 10. Aerial Warfare

The warrior woman rushed into the midst of the wolflings, brandishing her flashing blade.

Lewis realised, from his previous adventures among the Norse gods, that she must be one of the Valkyries, Odin's personal guards.

The wolflings gave way before the fury of her assault, opening an aisle between her and Loki.

Astonishingly, his face broke into a beaming smile. "Sigurda – baby!" he exclaimed happily.

"Hold your tongue, base villain!" the warrior woman commanded. She strode up to him and pressed the point of her sword to Loki's chest.

Loki raised his hands in surrender. "You're looking good, sweetheart," he said.

"Do not waste your honeyed words on me, trickster," Sigurda answered through gritted teeth.

"Come on, sugar," Loki coaxed, "don't pretend you haven't got feelings for me."

"All you shall feel from me is my wrath," Sigurda

responded frostily. "That, and the keen edge of my blade."

"Oh, don't be like that," Loki pleaded. "Remember how I always promised you I'd amount to something? Well, now I'm the boss of the whole show."

Sigurda glanced around and curled her lip contemptuously. "You are a shabby clown presiding over a pauper's court," she sneered.

"Okay, it's not much to look at right now," Loki admitted, "but wait till I've had time to fix it up a bit."

Sigurda transferred her attention to the prisoners. "Are you the Ringwearers?" she demanded.

In spite of her warlike manner, she seemed to be on their side, so Greg, Susie and Lewis all nodded and showed off their rings.

Turning back to Loki, Sigurda raised her sword point to his throat. "Bid your bestial guards withdraw," she ordered, "else I shall separate your head from your shoulders."

Loki sighed resignedly. "Better ease off, boys," he told the wolflings.

As the guards backed away, Sigurda's eye lighted on the crystal shard. She stiffened. "What vile mischief have you unleashed now?" she demanded of Loki. "That rock pulses with pure wickedness."

"Don't worry about it, sugar," soothed Loki. "I've got everything under control."

Lewis could tell Loki wasn't as confident as he was trying to appear.

The Viking god's jaw dropped as the crystal rose into the air and began to revolve. It grew larger and new facets spread across its face, throwing off glints of lurid light.

"You fool!" Sigurda raged at Loki. "This is beyond your control!"

Whipping away from Loki, she struck the crystal a resounding blow with her sword. The impact reverberated across the room like the clang of an enormous bell, but it appeared to have no effect on the shard. The crystal rose higher and spun more furiously, throwing off bolts of multicoloured lightning in all directions.

"Hit the deck!" cried Dave the Lobster, throwing himself flat.

A shrill whine ripped through the air. Streaks of energy played over the walls. Lewis flung himself to the floor as a spear of electricity sizzled past him, blasting the cycle helmet off the wall above his head.

The whine grew more piercing, driving the wolflings into a frenzy of terror. Dropping their swords, they clutched their ears and dived for cover under tables and chairs. Loki ducked behind his crudely painted throne as a bolt of energy smacked into the wall and set fire to one of the flags.

"Keep your head down, Spinny!" Greg cried as he and Susie crouched low to avoid the fireworks.

Unmoved by the chaos, Sigurda snatched Lewis to his feet and pointed to the open door with her sword. "Ringwearers, we must away!" she commanded. "I will act as rearguard."

"Any place has got to be better than here," said Susie.

Grabbing hold of Dave and Lewis, she and Greg made a dash for the door. Together they spilled into the hallway and pulled up short at the sight of the two police officers.

Iona and Kenny were guarding the exit with the same glazed look in their eyes. Iona signalled them to halt. "Please remain calm," she said flatly.

"The emergency services have everything under control," stated Kenny in the same tone.

Sigurda came barging out of Loki's throne room. "To the rooftop!" she ordered, leading the way upstairs.

"But we'll be trapped up there," Greg protested.

"Never argue with a woman holding a sword," said Susie, shoving him towards the stairway.

They all pounded up the steps after the Valkyrie.

"This is turning out to be quite a day," panted Dave the Lobster.

At the top of the stairs, Sigurda led them down a short passage and through another door. This opened into a storeroom full of cleaning supplies, spare chairs and rolled-up carpets, with an open skylight in the roof.

Susie looked up. "Is that the way you got in?" she asked Sigurda.

The Valkyrie nodded curtly.

"Crikey, that's some drop!" said Dave the Lobster. "You must be really fit."

From the direction of the stairwell came guttural growls and the heavy scuffle of clawed feet.

"Secure the door!" ordered Sigurda. "Loki's minions will soon be upon us."

With the help of the others, she braced the door shut with a folding chair and couple of broom handles just before the wolflings started banging on the panels.

Greg cast a sceptical glance at the skylight. "If you're expecting us to get out that way," he told Sigurda, "I hope you've brought jetpacks."

"I have already planned our escape," said Sigurda, pulling a lightweight aluminium ladder out of a far corner. She set it up under the skylight as the door began to crack under the wolflings' assault.

"Go quickly!" Sigurda ordered. "I shall hold them off."

Susie raced nimbly up the ladder and disappeared from view. Lewis hurried after with Dave the Lobster and Greg right behind.

Susie peered down to see Sigurda scrambling up the ladder just as the wolflings burst into the room.

They rushed in and toppled the ladder. But as it fell, Sigurda launched herself upward like an Olympic gymnast. She caught the frame of the skylight and swung herself to safety, landing on her feet beside the others.

"Blimey!" Dave the Lobster exclaimed. "What a performance!"

A chorus of frustrated howls issued from below.

"We must away before those reckless beasts think to copy our escape," said Sigurda. She threw back her head and gave a trilling whistle.

From somewhere above came an answer that sounded like the whinny of a large horse. Lewis looked up and gasped in wonder.

Descending out of the sky was a great white stallion, held aloft by a magnificent pair of feathered wings. He was harnessed to a two-wheeled chariot, which floated along behind him, as light as a leaf in the wind.

"Are you guys seeing what I'm seeing?" breathed Dave the Lobster.

"Just go with it," Susie told him.

The flying horse alighted on the roof and bowed his head to Sigurda. She caught hold of the stallion's luxuriant mane and swung herself onto his broad back. "Into the chariot!" she commanded.

They all leapt aboard as a loud metallic clatter warned them that the wolflings were replacing the ladder.

Sigurda clapped her heels to the stallion's powerful flanks. "Fly, Rimfaxi!" she cried.

Rearing back on powerful haunches, the great horse spread his wings and vaulted into the air. The wolflings piled onto the roof and howled at the sight of their quarry escaping into the clouds.

Lewis' stomach lurched violently as they made their speedy ascent. Clutching at the sides of the chariot, he groaned, "I think I'm going to be sick."

Susie whooped with glee. "This is *amazing*! Better than a roller coaster."

St Andrews was spread out beneath them, a patchwork of rooftops and gardens. Beyond the West Sands, Lewis saw a monstrous sea serpent rear up out of the waters of St Andrews Bay then dive back down with a colossal splash. The chariot swung round and swooped over the arching West Port – all that remained of the town's medieval walls.

Lewis stared out beyond the boundaries of the town and saw that the farmlands of Fife had been replaced by a far-flung wilderness of dark trees, broken here and there by stony ridges and gleaming lakes. To the far west rose a lofty snow-capped peak. Lewis recognised it as the mountain that had appeared on the screen at the museum.

Just then there came a piercing screech and they saw Loki's giant hawk plunging out of the clouds towards them.

"That dirty great budgie!" Greg exclaimed.

"It is Falkior, the hunting bird of Loki," said Sigurda grimly. She drew her sword. "Brace yourselves for battle."

The bird of prey sped towards them, its wicked claws extended to attack. Sigurda directed her mount sharply downward and the hawk shot over their heads in a rush of air.

Rimfaxi flew on, drawing the chariot out over the wooded landscape of Vanaheim. Vast crags of grey rock thrust upward like grasping fingers and the stallion climbed desperately to avoid the obstacles.

Suddenly the chariot wheels glanced off a rocky pinnacle and the three passengers were jolted off their feet.

With a cry of alarm Dave the Lobster lost his grip and toppled over the side.

"Dave!" Lewis yelled, stretching a helpless hand towards the marine biologist as he plummeted to earth. Right below them was a small lake where Dave splashed down before disappearing behind tall trees.

"Will he be okay?" Susie asked anxiously.

"I'm sure he can swim," said Lewis. "Like a lobster probably."

"Look, if we carry out this mission," said Greg, "Odin will rescue the fish guy from wherever he ends up. Right, Sigurda?"

"You speak the truth, Ringwearer. We cannot stop to help your friend now, but we shall return this way. If he acts with valour, he will come to no harm."

They were all struck dumb by the sight of the huge hawk Falkior rushing at them again. This time it struck home, gashing the stallion's right wing in a spray of blood. With a curse, Sigurda stabbed her sword at the bird but caught only empty air as it wheeled away.

Falkior let out a squawk of triumph and glided over the treetops, seeking an angle from which to resume its attack.

Sigurda patted the horse's neck. "You will pay for that, Falkior, blood for blood!" she swore.

Now the great hawk came at them head-on. Sigurda steered her brave mount directly at the enemy, then, at the last instant, pulled back on the reins to climb above the swooping bird. She threw herself out of the saddle, one hand gripping tightly to the shaggy mane, and swung under the great horse's neck. With her other arm she swept her sword downward and slashed it across Falkior's back as it passed below. The bird of prey let out a screech of agony as Sigurda swung herself around to the other side of her mount and back up into the saddle.

With a bloody gash down its back, Falkior beat a rapid retreat to St Andrews.

The three youngsters gave a cheer.

"Sigurda, that was amazing!" Susie enthused.

"Our victory has come at a price," said Sigurda, casting a pitying eye over Rimfaxi's bloodied wing. The horse was losing height as the deep wound drained the strength from his mighty body. Sigurda struggled to keep him on a straight course, her eyes scanning the forest below for a safe spot to set down.

Lewis, Greg and Susie clung desperately to the sides of the chariot as they spiralled steeply downward and the forest rushed up to meet them.

"Crash landing!" Greg exclaimed.

# 11. The Ironwood

They ploughed down through a dense covering of leaves and branches to hit the ground with a jarring crash. The chariot broke apart, spilling the three passengers out onto the mossy ground. Startled birds flew off in every direction, squawking in panic.

Only when his dizziness had passed did Lewis realise that he was alive and neither his arms nor legs were broken. Susie caught his hand and pulled him to his feet beside her. Greg was already up and stamping on the ground, as if to make sure it was really solid.

Rimfaxi had staggered away from the wreckage of the chariot and collapsed beneath a rocky overhang. Sigurda knelt beside him, stroking his mane and applying a patch of blue moss to his wounded wing.

She looked up at the three youngsters as they joined her. "Ringwearers," she said, "know that I am Sigurda, daughter of Oyunn, captain of the Valkyries, the warrior guard of Lord Odin."

"I'm Susie," Susie answered, "daughter of Theresa, and these guys are Greg and Lewis."

"Sons of Alan," Lewis added.

"Is your horse badly hurt?" asked Greg.

"His wounds are not mortal," said Sigurda, "but he needs rest in order to heal."

"Is there anything we can do to help?" asked Lewis.

Sigurda handed her helmet to Susie. "Use this to fetch water," she said. "There is a pool on the other side of those rocks." She plucked off a piece of the moss and handed it to the boys. "Gather as much of this as you can find," she said. "It has healing properties and will speed Rimfaxi's recovery."

Greg and Lewis stripped as much moss as they could from boulders and logs and carried it back to Sigurda. The Valkyrie used the water Susie brought to wash the wound then dressed it with moss.

"Shouldn't we go and look for Dave?" Lewis suggested. He was worried about the scientist, alone in this vast, strange woodland.

Sigurda shook her head firmly. "Time presses too heavily upon us."

"Oh, great!" said Greg. "So time is trying to squash us too. I suppose Loki is chasing after us."

"That may be," said Sigurda, "but the more urgent matter is our quest."

Lewis felt his stomach sink. "A quest?"

"Great!" said Susie eagerly. "Tell us all about it, Sigurda."

Sigurda stroked the horse's neck soothingly as she spoke.

"When Loki escaped from the Ginnungagap," she began, "he brought with him a jewel that allowed him to draw on ancient magical energies. You have seen its powers."

"Loki said it was a shard from the heart of Ymir," said Lewis.

Sigurda's eyes grew wide. "Ymir! He yet lives?"

"According to Loki he does," said Lewis. He reported everything Loki had told them.

Sigurda heard him out, and nodded grimly. "There are many stories of how the universe was born," she said, "but through them all runs a tale of the destroyer, the one who despises all life but his own. That one is Ymir, the dark shadow of creation, the lord of death."

"He's definitely scared the pants off Loki," said Greg.

"The trickster used Ymir's unholy power to seize your earthly town and with it displace the golden city of Asgard. Rimfaxi and I were on a mission far away when Lord Odin contacted me by means of the Nornstone, a mystic jewel in the pommel of my sword.

"By the foresight his godly power grants him," Sigurda continued, "Odin was warned of the destruction to come. Using the power of his Odinstaff, he escaped the golden city mere instants before Loki carried out his enchantment. He had just enough time to cast a spell that would preserve Asgard and conceal it in a place of safety where Loki would not find it."

"Can you use this Nornstone again to ask Odin where he's hidden it?" asked Susie.

Sigurda displayed the pommel of her sword. Only a blackened hollow remained where the jewel had been fixed. "The powerful magical energies destroyed the gem," she explained.

"Just like they blew up our TV," said Greg.

"Loki does not know that Asgard is safe," said Sigurda. "But the strain of casting such a powerful spell shattered Lord Odin's staff, breaking it into three pieces and scattering them across Vanaheim."

"So where is Odin?" asked Lewis.

"Without his staff and with his power depleted by the rescue of Asgard, he took refuge deep inside Mount Daggerflash," said Sigurda, "which towers above the western border of our land. He closed the walls of the mountain about him, so that Loki would be unable to detect his presence."

"That's what Odin was trying to tell us," Susie realised. "He didn't want us to find a dagger, he wanted us to find the mountain, Mount Daggerflash."

"So that will be the mountain he showed us on the monitor at the museum," said Greg.

"That's right," said Lewis. "I saw that same mountain when we were up in the sky."

"Odin cannot free himself from the mountain without his magical staff," said Sigurda. "He instructed me that the three Ringwearers would have the means to recover his staff and bring it to him."

"And how are we meant to do that?" asked Greg. "I don't suppose he left an instruction manual?"

"We must make our way towards Mount Daggerflash," said Sigurda, pointing decisively to the west, "and hope that the fates will deliver the three broken pieces into our hands."

"In other words we'll do what we usually do," said Greg. "Make it up as we go along."

Sigurda stroked her horse's mane. "Rimfaxi must rest here until he recovers," she said. "We shall continue our journey on foot."

"What? Without food?" Greg objected.

"You will find provisions aboard the chariot," Sigurda replied.

While she tended the wounded horse, Susie, Greg and Lewis searched the wreckage of the chariot. They salvaged five water flasks and a pouch with half a dozen apples in it.

"There are many streams here in the Ironwood from which the flasks can be filled," said Sigurda. "And these apples are from the orchard of Idunna."

"That sounds nice," said Greg, "but a few apples won't last us long."

"Share them out and try them," said Sigurda.

The apples were bright green with a golden sheen. They took one each and bit into it. It was the most delicious thing Lewis had ever tasted, sweet and nourishing. Before he knew what he was doing he had munched down half the apple.

"Mmm," said Susie. "It's nearly as good as a Mars ice-cream bar."

"It's delicious," Lewis admitted, "but like Greg said, they won't last long."

"Will they not?" countered Sigurda. "Just look at them."

Lewis examined his apple and saw to his astonishment that it was completely whole, as if he hadn't taken a single bite. And yet his stomach felt full from what he had eaten.

"The apples of Idunna renew themselves and can never be entirely consumed," Sigurda informed them.

Leaving an apple with Rimfaxi, they set out on their westward trek.

"I couldn't help noticing, Sigurda," said Susie, as they walked through the trees, "that you and Loki seem to know each other kind of well."

Sigurda grimaced uncomfortably and her fingers tightened around the hilt of her sword.

"It is true," she said, "that in an age long past he did woo me with precious gifts and sweet blandishments."

Greg's brow furrowed. "What is she saying?"

Susie lowered her voice and spoke confidentially. "She's saying that they used to *date*."

"You mean Loki used to be her *boyfriend*?" Lewis exclaimed.

"For the briefest moment of time," Sigurda protested through gritted teeth. "The merest blink in which an enemy blade might elude one's guard and penetrate the chink in ill-fashioned armour."

"She says it's a mistake anybody could have made," Susie explained.

Sigurda turned away from them and stomped off through the trees.

"She seems a bit touchy," said Lewis. "I think we'd better change the subject."

"Yes, before she shuts us up with her sword," Greg agreed.

As they walked through the dense woodland, branches kept snagging on Lewis' jumper and he stubbed his shoes on thick tree roots.

"To think, this day started out just fine," he complained. "I was going to catch microscopic sea life at the harbour and write a really interesting report about it. Loki has completely messed that up."

"Look on the bright side, Lewis," Greg encouraged him. "If you go down to the harbour now, instead of catching tadpoles you can probably net a giant octopus."

"That's not much of a comfort," said Lewis unhappily.

They had been walking for about an hour when they emerged from the trees to find themselves standing right on the edge of a deep crevasse. From far below, where the sunlight didn't reach, they could hear the roaring torrent of a mighty river.

Susie stared at the wide chasm, which seemed to divide the land in half as though cleaved apart by a gigantic axe. There appeared to be no way across.

"You know," she said, "there are times you could really do with a flying horse."

# 12. THE DRAGON BRIDGE

"The Utgard Chasm!" Sigurda exclaimed. "I was not expecting this."

"What do you mean you weren't expecting it?" said Greg. "This is your country, isn't it?"

"In supplanting golden Asgard with your earthly town," said Sigurda, "Loki has thrown the entire land into disarray, confounding its myriad elements."

"What's she saying?" Greg grunted.

"She says the geography of Vanaheim is all mixed up because of what Loki's done," Susie translated.

"Like chucking a rock into a pond," said Lewis. "By dropping St Andrews in the middle of Vanaheim, Loki's sent ripples out over the whole country."

"Okay, I get that," said Greg. "Why didn't she just say so instead of spouting all that gobbledygook?"

"She's a warrior maid of Asgard," said Susie. "You can't expect her to speak like somebody out of River City."

"Loki makes havoc where he cannot have victory," said Sigurda, "like a petulant child who, finding a wooden puzzle too difficult to solve, hurls the pieces to the floor in anger."

Lewis gazed at the huge gulf. "So how do we get across?" he asked.

"We must find the dragon," Sigurda stated decisively. She set off at full stride northwards along the chasm's rim.

"Are you saying we have to fight a dragon before we can cross?" asked Greg, hurrying after.

"There is no need to fight," said Sigurda. "It is already slain."

Thick groves of pine trees and steep boulders forced their path away from the chasm as they struggled to keep up with Sigurda.

"So about this dragon..." said Lewis.

"What do you mean it's already slain?" Greg asked.

"It was Thor, the god of thunder, who slew him in an age long past," said Sigurda.

"An awful lot of stuff went on in these *ages long past*," said Greg.

Susie gave him a dig with her elbow. "Shh! I want to hear this!"

"In that time," Sigurda resumed, "the dragon Affnar dwelt in a cave at the bottom of this very chasm. When he heard travellers passing above, he would rise up from his hidden lair and devour them.

When Thor walked this ground seeking some means to cross over, Affnar ascended on his mighty wings and attacked the god of thunder. Long and furious was the struggle between them and many are the songs sung of it even to this day. At last Thor struck a mortal blow, splitting the dragon's skull with his hammer. Affnar fell dead and Thor crossed safely to the other side."

"How did killing the dragon get him across?" asked Susie.

"You shall see," Sigurda replied. "You shall see."

Lewis took a fresh bite from his apple. Perhaps it was the effect of the magical fruit, but he was starting to enjoy this wild country. The air was clean and filled with the scent of pine. The trees grew straight and proud, and the distant calls of unseen birds were like music floating on the breeze. There were no roads here, no phones, no computers. It felt as if his normal life were the fairy tale and this world of warriors and flying beasts the reality.

"Hey, look! There's something up ahead!" Susie announced.

She had spotted a row of greyish-white rocks laid out end-to-end, increasing in size as they curved away out of sight behind the trees.

"Stones wouldn't naturally lie like that," said Greg

as they drew closer. "Somebody must have put them there."

"That's not it," said Lewis. "I think they must be..."

"Bones!" said Susie.

"Bones?" Greg echoed. "But look at the size of them!"

When they reached the strange structure they could see that it was the skeletal tail of some immense beast, so long it stretched away out of sight among the shadows of the trees. Sigurda led them along the length of the huge tail until they came to the Utgard Chasm once more. The skeleton of a gigantic dragon was stretched right across the chasm.

On this side were the tail and hind legs, the claws of its enormous feet dug solidly into the earth. The dead monster's spine formed a bridge across the crevasse to where its front claws were dug in on either side of a skull as big as a house. From the centre of the skeleton, extending towards the sky, rose the bones of its wings, like the framework of a pair of vast sails.

"So this is the dead dragon," Susie gasped.

"Verily you speak in sooth, Susie," Sigurda confirmed.

"I didn't know you could speak Sooth, Spinny," Greg joked. "Have you been taking lessons?"

Susie silenced him with a jab in the ribs as Sigurda continued her story.

"As Affnar writhed in pain from the blow struck by Thor, he finally fell dead directly across the gap, affording the god of thunder easy passage."

"It reminds me of that whale skeleton in the Dundee museum," said Lewis.

"Yes, except this is twenty times bigger," said Greg, "and it's a dragon."

"Are you sure it's safe to cross?" Lewis asked.

"There is no safety on the warrior's path," said Sigurda.

"Thanks," said Greg. "That's really reassuring."

A sudden rustling in the woodland behind them made Sigurda spin around and draw her sword. She eyed the trees suspiciously.

"Ringwearers, make your way across," she instructed. "I shall guard the rear."

"I'll go first," said Susie, hopping up onto the tail. Like a gymnast on a balance beam, she moved rapidly up to where it joined the body.

"Take it easy, Spinny," Greg cautioned her. "Those bones are really old. They could easily fall apart."

"Greg, if this thing's been here for centuries, it's not likely to choose this moment to collapse, is it?" Susie pointed out.

"I'm just saying to be careful," said Greg.

"I'll send you a postcard from the other side."

Susie headed along the spine holding her arms straight out at her sides for balance. The bones shifted and creaked slightly under her feet but Susie didn't let that disturb her.

Since she was three she had been climbing up onto narrow walls and walking along them fearlessly, even when her anxious parents pleaded with her to come down. She knew that the secret was to concentrate on each step, then the next, and not think about anything else. Especially not about falling.

"You're next, Lewis," said Greg.

Lewis gazed along the length of the dragon skeleton and swallowed. It looked like an awfully long way. "Why me?" He hated how squeaky his voice sounded.

"Because you're the next lightest," said Greg. "We want as little weight as possible on the thing."

"That sounds sensible – for once," Lewis agreed unhappily.

He placed a tentative foot on the tail and took his first step. Then another.

"Come on, Lewis, speed it up," Greg urged.

Soon Lewis had taken his first steps over the chasm, his eyes firmly fixed on Susie, who was continuing to make confident progress far ahead. *Don't look down*, he told himself. *You'll be fine as long as you don't look down.*

As he reached the halfway point he saw Susie hop up onto the dragon's cracked skull. She walked lightly down its snout and jumped onto solid ground on the other side. Twirling about on the grass, she laughed in relief.

Now that Lewis was in the centre of the dragon's body, the great sail-like structures that had supported the wings rose up around him. He was sure he could see them moving. He tried to block out the crazy notion that the dragon was coming to life, like some sort of giant lizard zombie. It must just be the wind moving the ancient wings.

But it was still worrying.

It also prompted Lewis to wonder how a creature this massive had ever managed to fly. Perhaps the bones, for all their size, were hollow, so they didn't actually weigh much. That thought made him nervous. If the bones weren't solid, then maybe this whole structure was a lot more fragile than it appeared.

"Lewis, what are you stopping for?" came Greg's voice.

Lewis twisted his head around and saw that Greg had started out after him. Greg was heavier than Susie. Suppose the dragon bones were too light to support the two of them?

"I know what you're doing," said Greg accusingly. "You're thinking. Now cut that out and get moving."

Lewis turned his eyes away from Greg, but as he did so, he accidentally glanced down. The chasm seemed to fall away forever into black shadows where an unseen river dashed along, ready to sweep away the dead body of anyone who fell.

Immediately he started to sway, letting out a yelp as his arms whirled about in a desperate effort to maintain his balance.

"Lewis, you're fine," said Greg loudly. He tried to think of some really good words from his *Verbal Ninja* book to calm his brother down. "Maintain your composure and move with alacrity."

"Composure?" Lewis echoed. "Alacrity? Where did you get that from?"

"I'll tell you once we're on the other side," Greg told him with a laugh.

Lewis found himself laughing too, and once he took his mind off his fears, he found he could start walking again. The long bony spine actually felt quite firm beneath his feet.

His confidence was coming back – when it was abruptly shattered by a mighty roar.

Lewis and Greg both swivelled their heads to see what was going on behind them. Sigurda had just started out across the bridge when an immense bear with thick black fur came roaring out of the forest.

It reared up to full height, twice that of a man, and raised great paws above its head to show off savage claws. Then it dropped to all fours and bounded forward in pursuit of Sigurda. As it landed on the dragon bridge, the whole structure shook like it had been hit with a hammer.

"Steady, Lewis, steady!" Greg called.

But it was too late.

Lewis lost his balance and, with a startled squeal, he fell.

# 13. That Way and This Way

"Lewis!" Greg cried. He stretched out a hand but his brother was too far away to reach.

As he toppled from the dragon's spine Lewis bumped against one of the huge ribs and instinctively threw his arms around it. Fearfully he shut his eyes and slid down a short way before coming to a halt. Only when he had stopped moving did he dare to look around.

Greg was directly above him now, but too far off to reach. To his left he spotted Susie darting nimbly back down the spine to join Greg.

Sigurda had turned and was facing the bear, her sword drawn. The creature slashed at her with one claw, but she deflected the blow with her blade. Every time the bear lunged, the whole skeleton shook and Lewis had to cling on for dear life.

Above him Greg swayed but managed to keep his balance as he slipped off his light daypack. He lay down full length, holding one strap, and dangled the pack below him so the other strap was only a short distance above Lewis' head.

"Here, Lewis, grab on!" he said.

Lewis was terrified that if he let go of the rib with one hand, he would lose his grip and topple into empty space.

Susie lay down on the spine so that the top of her head was almost touching Greg's. She wriggled out of her daypack and lowered it in the same way, so there were two loops hanging just above Lewis.

"Grab hold of one, Lewis, then the other," said Susie. "We'll haul you up."

Lewis was just mustering the courage to make the attempt when the whole skeleton shook once more. The bear was taking another swipe at Sigurda, but the Valkyrie held her ground.

With all four of them on the dragon bridge, and a bear that probably weighed as much as all of them combined, Lewis was sure the bones would give way.

"Come on, Lewis!" Greg urged. "You can't hang around there all day."

"Hang around!" Lewis muttered. "That's a bad joke, even for you, Greg."

The risk involved in grabbing for the dangling backpack scared him a lot. But so did the knowledge that eventually he would lose his grip and plunge into the abyss.

"Lewis, I think you'd better move now," said Susie.

Lewis saw at once what she meant. The rib he was holding onto was breaking loose of the spine.

Lewis sucked in a deep breath. Taking his left hand off the long curved bone, he grabbed hold of the strap of Greg's pack. His other hand immediately slipped free and he dangled there, his feet kicking the empty air.

Taking a firm grip on the dragon's vertebrae, Susie slid herself further down so she could lower her pack closer to Lewis.

"Susie, be careful!" Greg exclaimed.

"Come on, Lewis, grab a hold!" Susie called.

His legs swinging in the air, Lewis stretched his right arm until it ached. He just managed to get his fingers over the strap of Susie's pack.

"Hold on tight, Lewis!" said Greg. "Come on, Spinny, heave!"

The two of them pulled hard and dragged Lewis panting and puffing up onto the spine beside them. They had barely stood up when another angry roar shook the bridge again. They threw themselves flat and clung on to the shaking spine.

This time, however, the bear halted its advance. It had noticed that each time it moved to attack the strangers, the bony surface beneath it rocked and swayed. The bear was not used to the ground behaving like this and found it unsettling. It decided that the intruders had learned their lesson and would not trespass on its territory again.

Carefully the bear moved backwards onto solid ground. Once the earth was firm beneath its feet again, it reared up to full height and delivered a final warning. Then it dropped down onto all fours and padded majestically back into the forest.

"Good riddance!" said Greg. "I don't think the bridge could *bear* his weight."

The three of them scrambled to their feet and Susie and Greg slung their packs over their shoulders.

Sigurda gestured at them with her sword. "Separate!" she ordered.

"She's right," said Lewis. "Standing all together, we're putting too much strain on the bridge."

Even as he spoke they could feel the bones bend under their weight with an ominous cracking sound. The rib Lewis had been clinging to came loose and plummeted into the chasm. It seemed like a long time before they heard it splash down in the river far below.

"I'm out of here," Susie announced, darting nimbly towards the dragon's head.

"On you go, Lewis," urged Greg, giving his brother a gentle shove to get him moving.

Once they were spread out the bridge stopped bending. Lewis felt better when he reached the neck and followed it up onto the crown of the dragon's huge head. He could see clearly the gaping crack Thor's hammer had made in the monster's skull. He passed between the round empty eye sockets, so big you could ride a bike through them, then hurried down the long snout to join Susie on solid ground. When he looked back, he saw the dragon's huge teeth grinning at him like two rows of gravestones.

Greg arrived shortly after him, looking flushed and relieved. "That was a bit hairy, eh?" he beamed.

"I hope there's a different route back," said Lewis.

"I'll be happy if we get back at all," said Susie. She glanced towards the distant peak of Mount Daggerflash. "It looks like we've still got a fair hike ahead of us."

Sigurda marched confidently over the dragon's skull as if she were strolling down a broad highway rather than a shaky bridge of bones.

"That is one peril behind us," she commented as she rejoined the others. "Who can say what further dangers yet lie in our path?"

"Could you not say something cheerful for a change?" Lewis complained. Sigurda clapped him on the shoulder. "Danger is meat and drink to a warrior, Lewis," she declared, "for how else are we to test our mettle?"

"I don't know," said Lewis. "Sudoku? Table tennis?"

Sigurda laughed and led the way onward.

Directly ahead the crimson sun was sinking behind the distant peak of Mount Daggerflash. The mountain cast its long shadow across the land like a beckoning finger. As darkness fell the party made camp in a hollow surrounded by oak trees.

The three youngsters made beds for themselves out of moss and dead leaves and fell into an exhausted sleep. Sigurda slept sitting upright with her back against a boulder, her sword stabbed into the ground beside her within easy reach should anything startle her out of her slumber.

ᗠᗡᗠ ᗡᗠᗡ

A chorus of birds greeted the first golden sunbeams next morning. After a simple breakfast of apples and water, the travellers climbed out of the hollow and continued their westward journey.

The trees before them thinned out and they found themselves on the crest of a ridge that sloped gently down towards a broad and beautiful landscape. They saw hills and valleys, wide expanses of woodland, sudden shards of rock bursting out of the earth, and the silver traceries of streams and rivers.

"The land of Vanaheim," said Sigurda proudly, "though its features have been twisted by Loki's mischief."

"Hey, something's happening to my ring," said Lewis. "It's like there's a magnet pulling at it."

"I feel it too," said Greg.

"And me," said Susie. "It's yanking at my finger."

"They are drawing you to the separated parts of the Odinstaff," said Sigurda, "so that you might reunite them into one."

"My ring's pulling me that way," said Lewis, "to the north."

"Mine too," said Greg.

"Well, my ring's tugging me the other way," said Susie, pointing to the south.

"Which way are we supposed to go?" said Greg, rubbing his jaw.

"Two of the rings are pointing north," said Lewis, "so we should go that way first, then double back."

Sigurda shook her head. "Time flies swiftly and with each passing hour the danger grows. We must act quickly if we are to thwart the evil intents of Loki and Ymir."

"What's the plan then, Sigurda?" asked Susie.

"We shall divide our forces," Sigurda decided. "Lewis and Greg, you will travel northward. I will accompany Susie on the southward route."

"But how will we ever find each other again?" Lewis objected.

"Methinks once we've found two bits of the staff," said Susie, "the rings mayhap will lead us all to the third piece – eh, Sigurda?"

"Verily you speak in sooth, Susie," said Sigurda approvingly.

"Spinny, what are you talking like her for?" Greg asked sourly.

"I'm starting to get into it, Greg," Susie answered with a grin. "It's cool."

"So we'll all meet up at the third piece," said Lewis, "wherever it is." He had an uneasy feeling it wouldn't be that simple.

"Indeed, Lewis," Sigurda agreed, "then we shall resume our sundered fellowship."

Lewis and Greg glanced quizzically over at Susie, who could only shrug this time. "I guess it's sundering time then," she said. "Come on, Sigurda, let's see what's out there."

"Menfolk that way, womenfolk this way," said Sigurda. "May fortune smile upon you."

"Good luck to you too," said Greg.

As Susie set off with the Valkyrie for the south she looked round and waved. "You boys try to keep out of trouble!" she called.

"Right, Lewis, off we go," said Greg, starting towards the north.

Lewis slouched along unhappily beside him.

"What are you looking so glum about?" Greg asked.

"I should think that's obvious," said Lewis. "Who knows what sort of monsters are lurking out there. At least Susie's got a Valkyrie with her with a sword and everything."

"Not to worry, Lewis," said Greg, giving him an encouraging pat on the back. "You've got me."

# 14. A Pig in the Mud

"Well, Lewis, this is the life, eh?" said Greg.

They were strolling through a patch of elm trees towards a hill, which they hoped would give them a view of the route ahead. Lewis' eyes darted this way and that in expectation of an ambush.

"If by 'life' you mean 'the pits'," he said unhappily, "then yes. Loki's stolen our town, turned everybody into statues and we're lost in a weird country full of dragons, bears and wolves."

"It was a dead dragon, Lewis," Greg pointed out, "the bear ran away, and those wolf things of Loki's are as thick as Mum's Sunday custard."

"I'm still worried about Dave," said Lewis as they started up the hill. "How is he going to manage on his own?"

"He'll be fine," Greg assured him airily. "Didn't you say he's really brainy? He's probably nearly as smart as I am."

"If you're so smart," said Lewis, "do you know where we're going?"

"The rings know," said Greg. "It's just like following a satnav. Yours is still pulling you, right?"

"It gives my finger a tug now and then," Lewis answered. "I just hope we recognise this bit of magic staff when we find it."

"If we'd known they did this," said Greg, raising his hand to gaze at the Asgardian ring, "maybe we could have used them ages ago to find buried treasure and stuff."

"I don't think they work like that," said Lewis.

The top of the hill was covered in thick bramble bushes, and as they pushed through to the other side they came face to face with a Really Big Troll. They stopped dead in their tracks and stared at him. He stopped and stared back at them.

The troll was twice as tall as Lewis, with dull green skin. He had a huge, bulbous nose and tufts of red hair sprouted randomly from various points on his scalp. He wore a frayed leather tunic studded with metal discs and had a dirty blue rag tied around his head. He smiled, revealing rows of crooked teeth that looked like pebbles dug out of the ground.

"He looks pleased to see us," Greg muttered.

"Do you think that's a good thing?" Lewis murmured back.

The Really Big Troll stepped closer and squinted at the boys. "Ouat ee nid," he grunted.

"Sorry, I didn't quite get that," said Lewis.

"Frr teem," the troll explained.

"Whatever he's havering about," said Greg, "it looks like he wants us to stick around."

"Gum sonn," the Really Big Troll informed them amiably.

"We need to get away from him and find the staff," said Lewis anxiously.

Greg whipped a book out of his pocket and started flicking through the pages. "Maybe I can find some words in here to make him do what we want," he said.

Lewis wrinkled his nose doubtfully. "Is that the stupid book you bought, *The Verbal Samurai*?"

"*Ninja*, Lewis, *Ninja*," Greg corrected him. "A Samurai is something completely different."

He was still flipping pages when the Really Big Troll stretched down a massive paw and snatched the book out of his hands. He popped the paperback in his mouth, chewed twice, and swallowed it in a single gulp.

He made a face and grunted, "Sandwich too dry."

"Sandwich?" Greg echoed incredulously. "That was no sandwich, you great lump. That was the key to my future success."

"Hey, I understood what he said that time," said Lewis.

"When you get used to his grunting, it's not really that hard," Greg agreed.

The Really Big Troll beat a fist against his chest and declared, "Gruklob!"

"Hang on, I didn't catch that," said Greg.

"I think he's telling us his name," said Lewis.

The troll pounded his chest again and repeated, "Gruklob!"

"Nice to meet you, Gruklob," said Greg, pointing to himself and Lewis. "I'm *Bedbug* and this is my brother *Sickbag*."

"Bedbug, Sickbag," the troll repeated. He set off down the far side of the hill, beckoning the boys to follow.

"He doesn't seem like such a bad guy," said Greg, heading after the creature.

Lewis followed reluctantly. "Do you really think we should be going with him?"

"The rings are pulling that way, aren't they?" said Greg. "Besides, we're all pals now, aren't we, Gruklob?"

"Bedbug friend," the troll grunted. "Sickbag friend."

"What did you give us those stupid names for?" Lewis complained.

"We're operating undercover," said Greg, "like spies. All we need now is a pen that shoots poisoned darts and a car with an ejector seat."

At the bottom of the hill the troll led them through a maze of scraggy trees and mossy boulders to where another troll was waiting. He was even bigger than Gruklob with pale yellow skin and a crest of black hair sticking out of the top of his head. He also had a blue rag tied around his brow.

"Wer yu bin?" he asked Gruklob.

"Found two," Gruklob announced proudly, shoving the boys forward. "Bedbug and Sickbag."

"What do they want with us?" Lewis wondered. "Trolls don't eat people, do they?"

"I don't think so," said Greg, "but if you see a cooking pot, run for it."

The Even Bigger Troll stared at them. "Puny," he grunted, "but do." With that he turned and sauntered off through the trees.

Gruklob shoved the boys along after the Even Bigger Troll. He pointed at him and said, "Spudlug."

"Right, his name is Spudlug," said Greg.

"Team for game need..." Gruklob paused to count on his fingers. "Ten. Plus..." He paused to count his ears and his nose. "Three."

"Thirteen," Lewis piped up.

"Mugrash break leg kicking mountain, so can't play," said Gruklob. "Bograg pick fight with giant. Not see Bograg again. So need two. You."

"Did you hear that, Sickbag?" said Greg. "We're on the team."

"What team?" Lewis asked. "What do they expect us to do?"

Gruklob said no more but herded them along after Spudlug.

They followed Spudlug to a spot where crude stakes the height of a man had been driven into the ground. Stretched between them was a fence made of branches, woven grass and strips of tree bark, enclosing an area roughly the size of a football pitch. They were led through a gap in the crude fence and onto the enclosed field.

A couple of dozen trolls were milling about here, some wearing blue rags around their heads, others red. Standing in the middle of them all was a Very Old Troll with a huge purple nose and a wild mane of white hair. At the end of a leash he held a pig that was nosing about in the ground.

Spudlug approached the Very Old Troll and addressed him respectfully, lowering his head and bowing every few seconds. From the way he was gesturing in their direction, Lewis could tell he was talking about the two of them.

"It looks like they need that old guy's permission to let us on the team," said Greg. "I expect he's the referee."

"Is your ring still pulling?" asked Lewis.

"No, it's tingling now," said Greg. "Maybe that means

the staff piece is right here. We need to stick around till we find it."

After a short discussion, the Very Old Troll raised a hand in the air and declared, "Yes! Punies on blue team!"

"I wish they'd stop calling us puny," said Lewis.

"Stop being so sensitive," said Greg. "Keep your eyes peeled for the staff thingy."

The trolls in the blue headbands gave a ragged cheer and everyone headed to the centre of the field – a stretch of rough ground pitted with holes, many of which were filled with muddy water. Grassy hillocks rose up here and there with boulders and logs scattered all over.

Gruklob stood them before Spudlug, who slipped a length of blue rag over Lewis' brow and knotted it behind his head.

"Not so tight!" Lewis complained. "You'll cut off the circulation to my brain."

The troll performed the same operation on Greg, who grinned. "Now I actually feel like a ninja," he said.

"Sports!" Lewis moaned. "I never win at sports."

"Come on, Lewis," Greg said encouragingly, "remember that time you nearly beat me at table tennis."

"*Nearly*," Lewis repeated sourly.

"Rules simple," Gruklob explained. "Catch pig. Get pig in enemy circle. Keep pig in circle. Take enemy flag as sign of win."

Lewis looked up and down the field and saw that a circle of stones had been laid out at each end. There was a blue flag in one circle and a red flag in the other. When he looked at the red flag the tingling in his ring grew stronger.

"Greg, I think the red flagpole is what we're after," he said. "The piece of the staff!"

Greg squinted up the field and nodded. "That makes things simple. All we have to do is win the game and take the flag."

"Oh, right, that's no problem then," Lewis groaned.

"Lewis, it's just a game, okay? Like rugby."

"I hate rugby," said Lewis. "I nearly got killed that time they made me play it at school."

Both teams had now lined up facing each other. The Very Old Troll stood between them with the pig. Gruklob pushed the two boys into position among their teammates.

It started to rain and the trolls all cheered.

"I guess they like playing in mud," said Greg.

The Very Old Troll raised a fist in the air and yelled, "Ready for pig!"

Everybody tensed up as he released the animal. As soon as it was free the pig shot off, zigzagging across the field. With a savage roar, both teams set off in pursuit, bashing their opponents aside and slithering about in the mud.

"Come on, Lewis, let's go!" Greg urged, joining the chase.

Lewis tried to run after him but slipped and fell face-first in the mud. "Sports!" he groaned, spitting out a mouthful of mucky water. "I hate sports."

# 15. Island of Lost Souls

Hiking across the wild landscape of Vanaheim beside Sigurda, Susie was reminded of last year's Spinetti family holiday on the island of Mull. She and her older sister Toni (short for Antonia) had gone tramping through the heather and over rocky hills until they found a small loch, where they had dived in for a swim. Toni was working in America now. She had posted spectacular photos of the Grand Canyon on Facebook. Susie wondered if she would ever be able to tell Toni – or anyone – about her adventures in Vanaheim.

"Susie," said Sigurda, interrupting her reverie, "I can almost hear the thoughts buzzing in your head like bees in a hive."

"I was just thinking, Sigurda," said Susie, "that if I tell anybody about the adventures I've had, like when Thor came to St Andrews a few months back, or now here with you, they'd think I was cracked in the head. There's no way I can tell Father O'Dwyer at our church that I've met Thor and Loki."

"One was well met, I'll wager," said Sigurda, "the other not so."

"Yes, about that," said Susie. "How could you, you know, *hang out* with Loki? I mean, he's kind of a sleazeball, isn't he?"

"He is a rogue, that is certain," said Sigurda, "yet even a rogue may have his charms. In that long ago age I found him fair of face and sharp of wit, with always a merry jest upon his lips to lighten a weary heart."

"So you're saying he made you laugh."

"Yes, as when amid a storm of woe the clouds part and a shaft of golden sunlight gladdens the spirit. He was not like the others gods of Asgard, who are fixed in their ways. With him one always found the unexpected."

"Greg's like that too," said Susie. "He's kind of a goof, but next to him everybody else is boring. I mean, you don't ask for vanilla ice cream when there's chocolate-chip rum-and-raisin on the menu."

"Over time," Sigurda continued, "Loki was corrupted by ambition, growing both vain and selfish. His jests became bitter and cruel."

"So he went from being a clown to being a serious pain in the neck," said Susie sympathetically.

"I bade him depart my presence or feel the keen edge of my blade," Sigurda recalled. "And still, these many years later, he speaks as though some bond of caring yet exists between us."

"Guys, eh?" said Susie, rolling her eyes. "What are they like?"

They halted at the edge of a dark lake with a tree-covered island in the centre. Susie could see the stone towers of a castle poking up above the treetops.

"The ring's still nagging at me to go that way," she said, pointing across the lake. "Do you think we're supposed to go for a swim?"

"To do so would mean abandoning my weapons and armour here on the shore," said Sigurda ruefully, drumming her fingers on the hilt of her sword. "There must be some other means of crossing."

Even as she spoke, a splashing of oars caught their attention. A small boat was making its way towards them from the direction of the island. The boatman rowed steadily with his back to them, occasionally casting a disgruntled glance over his shoulder.

"It's a bit like phoning a taxi, isn't it?" said Susie. "You just think about how you need a boat, and zing, one shows up."

"It is Skarabeg the Boatman," said Sigurda. "Whenever a traveller in urgent need requires passage across water, Skarabeg and his boat appear, whether it be on a river, a lake or the tumultuous waves of the storm-tossed sea. That is the curse laid upon him."

"A curse?" said Susie. "How did that happen?"

"Once when Odin was walking the Earth in the guise of a very old man..." Sigurda began.

"In an age long past, I'll bet," Susie guessed.

"Indeed, in an age long past..." Sigurda agreed seriously. "Odin came to a great river where he begged passage of Skarabeg the Boatman. Skarabeg demanded payment in gold from the ragged old man.

"Odin protested that he had no wealth to share, but if Skarabeg gave him passage, he would pray to the gods to send him good fortune. Skarabeg laughed harshly and declared that prayers were of no value to him, whether they be to Odin or any other god.

"Angered by these arrogant words, Odin threw off his cloak and revealed his true identity as king of the gods. To punish the boatman for his selfish arrogance, he laid this curse on him. He and his boat would appear on lakes, rivers or at sea, wherever a traveller in need required passage. Skarabeg would be compelled to serve without payment, and so do penance for insulting the gods."

When the boat bumped up against the shore Susie saw that Skarabeg was a small, hunched figure with a round turnip of a face. His arms were thick and muscular from years of pulling on the oars.

"Hail, Skarabeg the Boatman," Sigurda greeted him. "We demand passage in accordance with the decree of Odin."

"Right, so you know me," Skarabeg retorted ungraciously. "Get in if you're coming."

Susie and Sigurda had barely settled into the boat when Skarabeg pulled abruptly away from the shore with a powerful heave on the oars.

"Hey!" cried Susie, grabbing the edge to steady herself. "I nearly went over there."

"I'm a busy man," Skarabeg informed her. "I can't wait around all day for you to make yourself comfortable."

Susie turned to Sigurda. "Cursing him doesn't seem to have improved his personality."

"Skarabeg, who dwells in yon island castle?" Sigurda asked the disgruntled man.

"Odin's curse forces me to give you passage," Skarabeg sneered, "but I'm not your travel guide. Find out for yourself."

A long shape passed under the boat, undulating through the murky water.

Susie peered over the side and wrinkled her nose. "There's all sorts of things squiggling about down there," she observed. "I don't suppose there's any point asking old Skarabeg what they are."

"I hope one of them jumps into the boat and bites you," Skarabeg snapped.

"You know, my cousin George is a taxi driver," said Susie, "and he's a lot nicer than you."

Skarabeg ignored her and carried on rowing.

"We went across Loch Ness in a boat once," said Susie. "I spent the whole time looking for the monster but never spotted it."

They struck the island shore with a jolt that almost threw Susie out of her seat.

"Thanks for the friendly chat," she said to Skarabeg as they climbed out, "and the soft landing."

The boatman hunched over his oars and a nasty smirk passed across his thin lips. "I'll wait here for you," he said. "Only for an hour, mind. If you're not back by then, you won't be coming back."

"What do you mean by that?" Susie asked him sharply.

Skarabeg shrugged. "I'm just saying; that's all."

"Waste no more time with him," said Sigurda. "We must be about our business."

A path of flat, crooked stones led through the trees. They followed it to the centre of the island where a craggy grey castle rose up. Its crumbling towers soared upward, like rocky fingers stabbing at the sky. Ivy crawled over the walls and wound itself around the battlements, as though trying to drag the whole structure down into the earth.

"This was definitely built in an age long past," said Susie. "I doubt anybody lives here now."

A pair of wooden doors, broken loose from their hinges and pitted with holes, hung askew in the arched entrance. As she passed between them, Sigurda drew her sword. "We must be prepared for any danger," she said.

"I wish I had my hockey stick," said Susie, following her inside.

"Hockey stick?" Sigurda repeated.

"I use it for ice hockey," said Susie, "when I'm playing for my team the Fife Flames."

"Ah, in a contest of skill and courage," said Sigurda.

"That's right," Susie enthused. "It's a Bearlander carbon and fibreglass AX3 with a super-low kick-point. It's a beaut."

From ahead came an eerie sound, like many voices moaning. They entered a great hall where sunlight filtered through the long, crumbling windows.

The place smelled of mildew and dust. Scattered about were tables and chairs, all broken and rotted with age. A wooden shield studded with rusted metal was fixed to one wall. Facing it on the other was the horned skull of some massive beast.

The flagstones had burst apart down the centre of the floor to expose a gaping fracture in the earth, from which emanated a sickly white light.

Susie felt a chill at the sight of it, as if somebody had opened a giant fridge right in front of her.

Suddenly a figure appeared out of the crack in the ground. It twisted up from the light, like a sheet blowing about in a gale. Susie saw it had arms and legs and a ghastly face with huge eyes. Its great gash of a mouth opened wide to let out a miserable howl. Then it turned and swooped off through one of the open doorways in the far wall.

"What was that?" Susie gasped. "What's going on?"

Sigurda's clenched her sword hilt tightly. "A crack has opened in the earth leading down to Niflheim, the land of the dead," she said. "Some of the ghosts have escaped."

"Ghosts?" Susie echoed unhappily. "Really? Ghosts?"

"The unquiet spirits of those who died without honour," Sigurda explained. "The brave who die in battle are carried to Valhalla, to dwell in joy and celebration, but those who flee danger are dragged down into Niflheim, the cold and misty land of death. Some of them accept their lot and pass their days in the bleak silence of the shadow realm. Others harbour bitterness against the living and escape to spread terror and torment."

"Look," Susie said nervously, "there's not much that scares me. But ghosts. Well, even when I didn't believe in them, they creeped me out. So now, well..." She shuddered.

"We must keep clear of that baleful light," said Sigurda, indicating the glowing crack with the point of her sword. "Which way are we bound?"

Susie felt the tug of the ring and pointed to a wide stone stairway ahead. "That way," she said. Her throat had gone so dry she could barely get the words out.

Sigurda started forward and Susie forced her feet to follow.

"Ghosts!" she muttered. "Why did it have to be ghosts? Why couldn't it be snakes or something?"

# 16. Match of the Day

The pig clearly had no intention of being caught. It rushed this way and that, darting between the legs of its pursuers, while they crashed into each other and splashed down in the mud.

"I'll bet that pig's been specially trained," said Greg as he and Lewis wound their way through the chaos, avoiding rocks, potholes and trolls.

"If you were being chased by a mob of big ugly trolls," said Lewis, "you wouldn't need to be trained to run away."

"Good point, Lewis. And if it's not trained, we should be able to outsmart it."

"Pigs are actually quite intelligent animals," said Lewis.

"You mean like the one that built a house out of bricks so the wolf couldn't blow it down?" said Greg scornfully. "That was just a story." Greg ran off, whooping, and swerved round a troll who tripped and fell right in front of him.

Lewis lost track of Greg as the troll rolled between them. He jumped on top of a flat stone and tried to catch his breath. Surveying the field, he saw the pig racing about, squeaking excitedly and trailing a posse of thundering trolls in its wake. He wondered if there was any way he and Greg could tilt this daft game in favour of their blue team.

If there was any strategy to this sport, it wasn't obvious. The trolls crashed into each other at random, flattening their teammates as often as their opponents. Their only hope of victory seemed to be falling on top of the pig by sheer luck. Whenever they did try to pounce on it, the pig dodged and left the hunters rolling in the muck.

The Very Old Troll stamped about the field waving his fist in the air and cheering on both teams. An air of authority seemed to surround him like an invisible shield, protecting him from the collisions going on all around him.

Lewis had no such protection, but being so much smaller than the trolls, they barely noticed him as he wove his way around the pitch. Even so, he took a few bruising knocks along the way. Desperate to escape the madness, he spotted a hollow log in the centre of the field and made straight for it. He dived inside and lay there, panting for breath.

A few moments of relief followed and Lewis considered hiding out there until the game was over. "If Susie were here, she'd catch that pig quick as a flash," he grumbled to himself. "Instead it's me tripping over my own feet and falling in the mud."

Then Greg's face appeared, peering into the log.

"Come on, Lewis! We'll never get our hands on the red team's flag this way."

"Couldn't we just steal it and run away?" Lewis suggested feebly.

"I'll bet the penalty for cheating is pretty severe," said Greg, "like being chucked into a pit of crocodiles or something. We'd better win it fair and square."

Lewis sighed. Much as he wanted to stay in hiding, he knew that Susie and Sigurda were counting on them. The fate of St Andrews and everyone in it depended on them getting the staff and freeing Odin.

He scrambled out to join his brother and wished he hadn't. The field was like a stormy sea rising and falling, with gangs of trolls crashing to the ground then jumping up again for a fresh round of mayhem.

Greg grabbed Lewis by the arm and hauled him along. "Look, there's the pig running around that bush," he said. "You stay here and I'll chase it towards you."

"What am I supposed to do when it gets here?" Lewis asked.

"Grab it round the neck and wrestle it to the ground, obviously," Greg replied.

"Obviously," Lewis muttered glumly as his brother raced off.

Greg caught up with the pig, waving his arms and yelling to drive it back to his brother. When Lewis saw the animal rushing towards him, he took a step backwards and fell right into a big, muddy hole.

"Yuggh!" he howled as his backside sank into the mud. "This is the worst!"

He was struggling to his feet when the pig came flying off the edge of the hole and landed right on top of him. Lewis was flattened as it walloped the breath out of him.

"Oh, you stupid beast!" he gasped, trying to push it off.

Suddenly he was aware that the pig was poking its snout into his pocket and snuffling excitedly.

"Here, get off!" Lewis exclaimed.

He shoved it back with one hand and reached the other into his pocket. He pulled out the apple from Idunna's orchard. With a delighted squeal, the pig jumped at it and took a bite.

"Now you cut that out!" Lewis warned, shoving the apple behind his back out of reach.

The pig guzzled down its piece of fruit then tried to get around Lewis for another bite.

Greg appeared, standing over the hole with a big grin on his face. "Great plan, Lewis!" said Greg. "You've got him hooked like a fish!"

"Get me out of here!" said Lewis, wriggling out from under the snuffling pig.

Greg pulled him out of the hole and the pig scrambled up after him, trying desperately for another bite of apple. Lewis kept it out of reach, realising the chance they now had.

"We can win this!" he told Greg. "Where's the flag?"

"That way," said Greg. He pointed and ran for the circle at the end of the field.

Lewis raced after, waving the apple above his head. He was aware of the tingling from his ring getting stronger the closer he came to the flag. "Come on, piggy! Come and get it!" he called.

The pig's eyes lit up as it dashed after him, snorting greedily. With the hungry animal in hot pursuit, the brothers wove their way through the bedlam.

A pair of trolls were wrestling on the ground right in their path. Greg leapt over them and Lewis swerved around them with the pig on his heels.

As soon as he reached the end of the field, Lewis threw himself down inside the circle of stones. The pig jumped on top of him. It pressed its snout into his hand and forced the apple loose.

Greg bounded onto the pig's back and pulled the apple loose of its eager jaws. With an angry snort the pig reared up and threw him to the ground.

"Don't let it have the apple," Lewis gasped, scrambling to his feet.

"I won't," said Greg with determination. "As long as we've got the apple he'll stay inside the circle."

The pig jumped on top of Greg and made a fresh assault on the delicious fruit.

Suddenly Lewis saw one of the red team thundering towards them, his arms outstretched to sweep up the pig. Before the opposing player could grab it, Gruklob came flying out of nowhere. He shoulder-charged the red troll and sent him sprawling face first into a pool of mud.

"The flag, Lewis!" Greg gasped as the pig managed to clamp its jaws around the apple. "Get the flag!"

Lewis scrambled to his feet, grabbed the flag, and pulled it out of the ground. As he waved it above his head, the entire blue team gathered around him and let out a raucous cheer.

The pig burped and squatted on the grass with a blissful smile on its snout.

"Hey, it's scoffed the whole thing!" Lewis moaned.

"It doesn't matter now," said Greg, clambering to his feet. He laid a congratulatory hand on his brother's shoulder. "We won. *You* won!"

"Yes, I did, didn't I," said Lewis. He couldn't help feeling a glow of triumph. Maybe sports weren't so bad after all.

The rain shower had passed and the sun came out, as if to celebrate.

The Very Old Troll patted both boys on the back hard enough to leave a bruise. "Punies win for blue!" he declared, to a huge cheer from all the trolls, who seemed to have forgotten they were on opposite teams only a minute ago.

Barrels of ale were rolled out and tankards made from rams' horns were passed around. The trolls filled their tankards and toasted each other, then they toasted the white-haired referee, then the pig, then Greg and Lewis, then the trees, and even the mud. Spudlug poured some ale into a bowl and set it down in front of the pig, which guzzled it down thirstily.

"Some game, eh, Lewis?" said Greg. "They should show it on *Match of the Day.*"

Greg accepted a flagon of ale from Gruklob and took a gulp that nearly choked him.

"It's like drinking dishwater!" he croaked, spitting out the foul mouthful.

"Come on," said Lewis. He pulled the red rag loose of the rod and tossed it aside. "While they're partying they won't notice us sneaking off."

They had no problem clambering over the flimsy fence, and dashed off through the woodland, elated with their success.

When they reached a clearing they paused to examine their prize.

"Not much to look at, is it?" said Greg. "It looks like an ordinary piece of wood."

"Maybe you need to switch it on," said Lewis, taking a firm grip on the rod. As his ring pressed against it, rows of runes lit up all down its length – symbols from the ancient Viking alphabet, signifying the power of the gods.

"That's more like it," said Greg. "Now we've got magic."

"I can feel it pulling me," said Lewis. "Just like the rings did."

"Of course," said Greg. "It's going to lead us to the next piece of the staff."

"Let's go then," said Lewis, hanging onto the rod and leading the way.

Gradually the power of the staff drew them along until they reached a grassy glade.

"What's going on?" asked Greg. "Why have we stopped?"

"It's not tugging any more," said Lewis. "I'm just getting a weird tingling sensation all down my arm."

149

"Say, do you feel the ground shaking?" asked Greg.

At that exact moment the earth gave way beneath them and they tumbled down into darkness.

# 17. Ghostbashers

Screeches and howls echoed throughout the derelict castle as Sigurda and Susie slowly climbed the stairs. Susie felt her skin crawl and it took all her nerve to keep going. Maybe these ghosts would turn out to be a trick pulled by some old janitor with hidden speakers and holographic projections. But she knew this wasn't a cartoon. These truly were spirits from the land of the dead.

"No wonder the folk that used to live here flitted some place else," she said.

A diaphanous shape, wavering like a reflection in water, swept down the steps towards them. Sigurda stiffened and Susie pulled away. The edge of a fluttering sleeve touched Susie's bare arm as the apparition passed. Her whole body shook as though a bucket of ice water had been dashed over her.

"Eeugh!" she cried. "That was nasty!"

The ghost floated on down the stairs and disappeared through an archway.

"They carry with them the deathly chill of the shadowy realm from which they have escaped," said Sigurda. It was impossible to imagine the Valkyrie being afraid, but Susie could tell she was definitely on edge.

"I would rather face a more fleshly foe," Sigurda said through gritted teeth, "no matter how large or ferocious. My well-forged steel is of little avail against phantoms."

"Yes, you might as well poke a stick at them for all the good it will do," Susie agreed. "But they can't really hurt us, can they? I mean they're not even solid. It's like they're made of smoke or gas or something."

"The wind that gusts down from the icy north is as insubstantial as they," said Sigurda, "yet it can freeze the blood in your veins."

"Yes, I've heard about people dying from cold," said Susie. "Brrr... I don't fancy that much."

At the top of the stairs they found a long hall stretching before them, the floor covered with the disintegrated remains of an ancient carpet. Here and there the floor had given way and they had to make their way carefully around the yawning holes. Above them parts of the roof had fallen in, admitting thin streamers of sunlight.

All down one wall were carvings of giants, trolls, dwarfs

and men, joined in battle, with axes falling on heads and arrows whizzing through the air. The opposite wall was carved with scenes of the sea, ships at full sail and serpents rising up from the depths with jaws wide open to devour the unsuspecting sailors. Interrupting the carvings were several open archways on both walls, leading to side passages that disappeared into a far-off gloom.

As they walked down the hall, ghosts emerged from the empty archways and swooped about them before vanishing back into the darkness. One of them hovered above the dusty floor for a few seconds then flew straight at Susie. She slapped a hand over her mouth to stifle a scream as the ghastly face leered at her, its horrid breath like an arctic blast. With a giggling laugh the apparition fluttered off and disappeared.

Susie lowered her hand and took a deep breath. "I wish Greg was here to say something funny," she gasped.

The prompting of the ring led her to a door in the far corner of the great hall. This opened onto a spiral stairway that twisted upward out of sight.

"This must be one of the towers," said Sigurda. "Let us ascend."

Some of the stones beneath their feet felt loose and Susie was half afraid that the whole stairway would collapse and bury them.

"The staff piece couldn't just be hanging by the front door, could it," she muttered. "No, that would be too easy."

"Take heart, Susie," Sigurda encouraged her. "We are nearly at the end of our quest."

"The ring is tingling like mad," said Susie as they reached a door at the top of the tower. "The staff must be in there."

Eager to get off the unsteady steps, she pulled at the door and it creaked open to reveal the room beyond. Most of the roof was gone, leaving it exposed to the sky. The floor was covered in cracks and looked like it might cave in at any moment.

But that wasn't the worst of it.

"Oh no!" Susie gasped.

A crowd of phantoms, too numerous to count, swarmed the chamber. They melted into each other and separated again, their pale, drawn faces distorting like images in a broken mirror.

Sigurda peered into the room, trying to see through the misty forms of the ghosts to the far side. "There is a hollow in the far wall," she said. "I can see the staff piece rests there."

"You've got good eyesight," said Susie. "It's like staring into a fog."

All at once the ghosts fixed the two intruders with

a hostile glare that made Susie think of the phrase, 'If looks could kill'. From their quivering lips came a horrendous howl that echoed off the walls.

"Ow! What a row!" Susie cried, reeling back and clamping her hands over her ears.

"The magical energy of the staff has drawn them here and they throng about it like moths round a flame," said Sigurda.

"Bad luck for us," said Susie. "I don't suppose they'd leave if we told them there was a Halloween party downstairs."

As if in answer to the suggestion, the ghosts glared at them and redoubled their eerie din.

"We must attempt to retrieve the staff," said Sigurda, "whatever the cost."

"Hang on, Sigurda," said Susie, placing a cautious hand on the Valkyrie's arm. "We'll never get through that lot without freezing to death."

"You speak in sooth," Sigurda agreed ruefully. "Before we reach the staff the blood will likely freeze in our veins and we will fall dead upon the floor." She stared grimly at the mob of ghosts. "Still, if that is our fate..."

"Look, Sigurda, do you want to die or do you want to get the staff?" Susie asked pointedly.

Sigurda pondered the question for a moment. "It would not be a glorious death," she concluded.

"No, it wouldn't," said Susie.

Sigurda shook her sword in agitation. "So what are we to do? What course is there to follow?"

"Methinks, Sigurda, that we verily need to use our brains," said Susie, "like Lewis would do if he was here." She rubbed her nose hard, as if that might stir up some ideas. "It seems to me, if they can freeze us to death like you say, why do they waste their time making faces and shrieking just to scare us?"

"I know not. It is the way of their kind."

Susie could feel an idea forming in her mind. "Think about it then. Since they feel really, really cold to us, maybe to them we're really, really hot."

"Such a thought had never occurred to me," said Sigurda, "but it carries the ring of truth."

"Sure, maybe touching us burns them, and that's why they never get too close."

"We might destroy some of them with our touch even as we succumb to their deathly chill, but how will that advance our quest?"

"If I'm right, they've as much reason to keep clear of us as we have to stay away from them. Sigurda, you said they were the spirits of... who again?"

"Those who died without honour," Sigurda answered with a sneer. "Base cowards and craven fools who ran from battle and hid from every danger."

"Well, if that's right," said Susie, "then surely they must be more scared of us than we are of them."

Sigurda's brow furrowed in thought. "There is wisdom in what you say, Susie. You and I are the ones with courage while they are the most spineless of beings."

"Right," said Susie with a grin, "so instead of letting them scare us, why don't we give them a fleg for a change?"

Sigurda matched Susie's grin with one of her own as she turned to face the howling mob of spectres. "Yes, we shall show them our mettle and see whether they stand their ground."

Susie fell into a skating crouch, as though she were out on the ice with her team, the Fife Flames, driving the puck towards the opposing goal with her Bearlander carbon and fibreglass AX3 hockey stick. She eyed the ghosts as though they were a line of defenders and the competitive fire blazed inside her.

"Fife Flames!" she yelled at the top of her lungs. "We own the ice!"

Sigurda raised her sword high above her head. "For the honour of Asgard!" she roared.

As their voices echoed around the room the screeches of the ghosts dwindled to whispers. The whole mob shrank back and cringed before the two warriors.

"Valkyries attack!" cried Sigurda.

"Let's have you then!" yelled Susie.

Together they charged, roaring their battle cries.

A squeal of terror broke from the quivering phantoms and they scattered in panic. Some slipped down cracks in the floor, some flew headlong out the windows, while others shot straight up through the gaping roof. In a matter of seconds every one of them had disappeared, leaving Susie and Sigurda side by side in the middle of the room.

Susie punched the air and yelled, "Kaboom!" which was how she always celebrated a goal. "Fife Flames one hundred – Scaredy-cat Ghosts nil!"

"They have fled, leaving us masters of the field," Sigurda agreed, surveying the room with satisfaction. "As when spearmen on foot, facing the charge of a mounted warrior, fling aside their weapons and flee in panic, leaving behind their honour along with their spears."

"I couldn't have put it better myself," laughed Susie. "Ghostbashers – that's us!"

Sigurda sheathed her sword and grabbed the plain piece of wood that was nestled in the alcove. Susie saw it was about as long as her arm and looked surprisingly ordinary.

"The first part of the quest is completed," said Sigurda. "Now we must resume our journey."

When they returned to the boat, Skarabeg scowled at them.

"Yes, it's us," Susie announced cheerfully. "Sorry we didn't get eaten by anything."

"The day's not over yet," Skarabeg retorted sullenly.

The passengers barely had time to settle into the boat before Skarabeg hauled on the oars and pulled away from the island.

"Hey, Sigurda, something funny's happened," said Susie. "I don't feel the ring pulling me any more."

"Is it not drawing you on to another piece of the staff?" said Sigurda.

"No, it's not. So how are we going to find our way?" Susie wondered. "Here, maybe you should let me see that stick."

Sigurda passed over the staff and Susie took it in her right hand. As soon as the ring on her finger pressed against the wood, a series of runes lit up down its whole length.

At the same time the boat jerked violently and went into a spin.

"Here, what's going on?" Skarabeg protested. He dug his oars into the water in a futile attempt to stop the rotation.

"Your ring has reawakened the dormant energies within the staff!" declared Sigurda.

"It looks like the Force is with us, Sigurda!" Susie exclaimed gleefully.

The spinning of the boat was starting to make her feel queasy when suddenly it shot off in a straight line across the lake, as though driven by an invisible engine.

"Here, you stop this right now!" howled Skarabeg. "I do the steering around here."

"Sorry, Skarabeg," said Susie. "It looks like we're going for a ride."

"The pieces of the staff are being drawn together by the magical energies contained within them," Sigurda surmised.

"I'd better keep a tight hold then," said Susie, gripping the stick firmly.

Skarabeg continued his complaints as they were carried into a river that flowed westward out of the lake. The steep banks flew by rapidly as the boat skipped over the water.

"Whee!" Susie cried. "This is like being in a speedboat!"

Up ahead the river divided and the boat swerved into the right fork.

"Here, is that a rock face up ahead?" said Susie. They were being carried unstoppably towards a solid cliff.

"No, no, no!" Skarabeg squealed. "You're going to wreck my boat!"

"Fear not," said Sigurda. "I spy a cave."

"You're right," said Susie. "The river flows right into it."

They flew directly into the mouth of a tunnel and downward into pitch darkness.

# 18. Deeper and Down

After only a short fall, Lewis and Greg landed in a soft pile of the earth that had given way beneath them.

Greg spat dirt out of his mouth. "Well, that was unexpected."

Lewis got up and brushed soil from his trousers. He bent down and poked around in the dislodged dirt until he found the rod, which had slipped from his fingers. He could barely see it in the faint light trickling down from above.

Greg got to his feet and gazed around him. They were in a narrow tunnel that ran in both directions. There was barely enough room for them to stand upright.

"Should we try to climb back up?" he wondered, glancing up at the hole above their heads.

"No, I think we're supposed to be here," said Lewis. "I think the rod made that hole open up."

"That's a fly trick, I must say," said Greg.

"It's pulling that way," said Lewis, pointing down the tunnel.

Greg squinted. "I can see a light. Let's go."

The tunnel slanted steeply downward and they soon discovered the source of the faint light. Set into the walls at irregular intervals were rocks the size of footballs that glowed with a bright orange radiance.

"Don't touch it!" Lewis warned as Greg stretched a hand towards one of them.

"Relax," said Greg, rubbing his fingers over the glowing rock. "It's not even warm. Funny that, eh?"

"Listen, do you hear something?" said Lewis.

From up ahead came the rumble and whirr of machinery.

"Sounds like the noises the rides make at the fair," said Greg, "but without all the laughing and screaming."

They carried on until the passage came to an end. Cutting across it was a larger tunnel. In the floor a pair of deep grooves stretched off to the left and right. Clumps of glowing rock illuminated the passage in both directions.

"Which way now?" Greg asked.

Before Lewis could answer there came a rattling rumble from the left. Without a word they both pulled back into the shadows and watched as a crazy contraption came hurtling past as fast as a speeding bicycle.

It was a cart with four metal wheels that slotted into the grooves in the floor. Standing in the cart were two small bearded men, each holding the end of a handle that they were pumping up and down. This seesaw motion seemed to be powering the wheels. With a rattle and a rush the machine flew past and disappeared down the tunnel.

"Who were those guys?" Greg wondered.

"I would guess that they're dwarfs," said Lewis. "From what I've read, they live underground, mining ore and forging things out of metal."

"I suppose we should go the same way," said Greg.

"That's what the rod says," answered Lewis.

"Keep your ears peeled for any more of those carriages," Greg warned. "I don't want to get squashed."

As they walked on, other grooved tunnels cut across this one, all of them echoing with the distant clatter of metal wheels. The passage widened into a circular space, with a large hole in the roof overhead. In the middle of the floor was a deep shaft plunging straight down into darkness, with only a narrow ledge running round the edge. Lewis and Greg shuffled carefully around, their backs pressed to the wall.

"Health-and-safety people would have nightmares about this place," said Lewis, who had at one time considered health and safety as a career.

Even as he spoke there was a rumbling up above and a wooden platform came hurtling down. It shot past them at an alarming speed and they saw three dwarfs clinging to the sides as the platform vanished into the gloom below.

"That is the most dangerous lift I've ever seen," said Lewis.

"This is a busy place," said Greg, "like a cross between a factory and a fairground."

Once they had made their way around the open lift shaft, they headed along another passage until they eventually emerged into a vast cavern as big as a football stadium. They walked cautiously along a ledge that was set halfway up the cavern wall.

Down below, a pool of flaming liquid blazed in the centre of the floor, fed by several streams that flowed down the sides of the cavern from cracks in the rock. Around the edge of the pool dwarfs with long ladles scooped up fiery globs and poured them into stone urns, which were carried off in wagons pulled by moles the size of ponies.

Lewis noticed that the dwarfs all wore caps of red, blue, green, yellow and purple, which seemed to indicate the jobs they had been assigned to. The caps varied in size from small and flat to tall and pointed. This he supposed marked out different ranks among the dwarfs, as the ones in the pointed caps seemed to be giving the orders.

Overhead, lit by glowing stones in the roof, buckets on ropes were being winched across the chamber by a system of pulleys. Like soldiers on the march they emerged from gaps in the stone wall to disappear through holes on the other side.

It was a relief when they reached the far side of the cavern and the safety of a tunnel whose close walls felt welcoming after shuffling along the edge of a fatal drop.

"You'd think somebody would have spotted us by now, wouldn't you?" said Greg.

"They're all so busy with their work," said Lewis, "they don't seem to be aware of anything else. You could probably drive a bus through here and nobody would notice."

Lewis led the way down a side tunnel, which brought them into a chamber that appeared to serve both as a storeroom and a workshop. The room was divided into sections by free-standing shelf units packed with ledgers, tools and lumps of metallic ore. These formed a maze as complex as the network of tunnels they had already passed through. Stone pillars supported the roof and above their heads was an array of criss-crossing wooden walkways.

The rod was twitching so insistently, Lewis was sure they were close to their goal. At the sound of voices ahead, they peeked around the edge of a stack of shelves and saw three dwarfs in pointed caps gathered around a table. In the centre of the table, perched on top of a brass framework, sat a piece of the Odinstaff. The dwarfs were examining it through a variety of lenses and multifaceted crystals. They were also bickering furiously, their voices as harsh as the angry jabbering of blackbirds.

One was slightly taller than the others, which meant he was about the height of Lewis' navel. His straggly beard trickled down to his belt buckle and he tugged at it as he spoke.

"I say we set fire to it and see what happens."

"And when you've turned it into a pile of ashes, what do we do then?" snapped the next tallest.

"I suppose you have a better idea rolling around in that rock sample you call a head," said the first dwarf.

"I don't know what you and Nodnol are arguing for, Fleebit," said the third dwarf. "After all, it's just a bit of wood."

"Do not disparage wood, Triptok," said Fleebit. "While it lacks the noble properties of metal or rock, it does have many uses."

"And this is no ordinary wood," said Nodnol. He leaned close to the rod and sniffed it. "Why, you can actually smell the magic on it."

"I'll thank you to keep your nose off my property," snapped Fleebit.

"Your property?" said Triptok. "I think not, Fleebit."

"I was the one who found the thing when it came tumbling down that hole," Fleebit pointed out.

"Yes, and I am the one who caught you trying to hide it under your bed," said Nodnol huffily. "As Senior Technician it is my job to examine the object and determine its nature."

"You are forgetting," Triptok interjected, "that as Cavern Supervisor, this whole business lies under my authority."

"I believe the ancient and venerable rule of 'finders keepers' trumps either of your supposed claims," Fleebit asserted haughtily.

"Well, if you are determined to make a dispute of it," said Triptok with a sniff, "we could always hold a committee meeting."

"Not another committee meeting," groaned Fleebit. "The last one dragged on for five days."

"And we still haven't caught up with the lost production," Nodnol added bitterly.

Lewis and Greg ducked back out of sight and conferred in whispers.

"Well, that's definitely a bit of the Odinstaff they've got," said Greg.

"So how are we going to get it off them?" Lewis wondered.

Greg looked about him and grinned as his eye lighted on a pair of pointed purple caps lying on a nearby table. "Don't worry about that, Lewis," he said, grabbing the caps. "Just you follow my lead."

He stuck one of the caps on Lewis' head and put the other on himself. He then stepped out of cover and strode boldly towards the three dwarfs, waving at Lewis to follow. Lewis groaned and went after him.

"It's alright, guys," Greg announced heartily. "We'll take over from here."

The three dwarfs turned and stared quizzically at the newcomers.

"And who might you be?" Fleebit demanded.

"We're Earwax and Dustbin," said Greg, "from Central Office."

"Central Office?" said Nodnol.

"That's right, isn't it, Dustbin?" said Greg, jogging Lewis with his elbow.

Lewis nodded, wishing he were a million miles away from this latest of Greg's scams.

The dwarfs crowded together and conferred.

"What manner of creatures are these?" said Fleebit. "Surely not dwarfs."

"They look like humans," said Nodnol.

"And yet they are wearing the official caps of Senior Administrators," Triptok pointed out. "We must respect that."

"We're here from Central HQ," Greg pressed on, "the Command Centre. We've been sent by the head honchos to collect all magic sticks."

"By what authority do you do this?" Triptok enquired.

"We are Senior Officers in the Department For Measuring Things To See How Long They Are," Greg informed him. "So hand that stick over and we'll be on our way."

He took a step towards the table, but the three dwarfs closed ranks to block his way.

"Really, this is most irregular," said Fleebit.

"We need to see your documentation," said Nodnol.

"Documentation?" said Greg. "Are you kidding?"

"You must have an Interdepartmental Authorisation Scroll," Triptok insisted.

"Come on, Dustbin," Greg said to Lewis, "I'll bet you've got some kind of official document on you."

"Er... yes, Earfluff," said Lewis, poking around in his pocket.

"Earwax," Greg corrected him. "You keep looking. You'll see, lads," he told the dwarfs, "he'll have it on him somewhere."

While the dwarfs watched Lewis expectantly, Greg inched closer to the final piece of the staff.

Fleebit whipped out a short sword and pointed it at Greg. "You stay right there, Earwax," he warned. "There are serious penalties for impersonating an official of the Subterranean Administration."

Greg raised his hands in a peaceful gesture. "Don't be like that," he said. "We're the real deal, one hundred per cent genuine – you take it from me."

Lewis was still playing for time searching through his pockets for the non-existent document. He was wondering how long he could keep this up when he spotted something that made him start. Behind the backs of the dwarfs a rope was snaking down towards the table from an overhead walkway.

His eyes widened as a familiar figure slid down the rope and snatched the wooden rod from its stand.

"Susie!" Lewis gasped.

Too late, the dwarfs spun round to see the girl clamber back up the rope to where Sigurda waited on the walkway.

"Get a move on, you two!" Susie called to the boys. "There's a ladder over there!"

# 19. Up, Up and Away!

The ladder Susie was pointing to ran straight up to one of the overhead walkways. Lewis and Greg tossed aside their hats and made a dash for it. Nodnol pulled out a horn and blew a single harsh note. Within seconds answering blasts were echoing down the subterranean tunnels.

"Sounds like that was the alarm," said Greg, leaping onto the ladder and scrambling up.

Lewis hurried after him up to the wooden walkway where Susie and Sigurda were waiting.

"Spinny," said Greg, "you are just the best at showing up out of the blue."

"I know, Greg," Susie grinned. "That's number three on the list of reasons why you love me."

"Love?" Greg exclaimed in horror. "Spinny, if I still had my ninja book, I'd have a few choice words for you!"

"This way!" Sigurda commanded.

She ran along the walkway through an opening and into a long tunnel with the three youngsters close on her heels. Horn blasts continued to echo all around mixed with angry dwarf voices and the patter of running feet.

"How do we get out of here?" asked Lewis. "We must be nearly a mile underground."

"Don't worry about it," said Susie. "We already scoped out an exit."

At the end of the tunnel a wooden cage was suspended inside a shaft. They bounded into it and Susie hauled the gate shut behind them.

Sigurda pulled a lever in the wall and suddenly a pair of boulders dropped down on either side of them. These were attached to the cage by ropes and pulleys and the dropping weights sent them rocketing up the shaft towards the surface.

"How did you get here anyway?" Lewis asked as the cage rattled up the passage.

"Well," said Susie, "to cut a long story short, after we got this piece of the staff" – she showed them the section she and Sigurda had already obtained – "it took control of the boat we were in and sent us zooming into an underground lake lit up by orange rocks. As soon as Sigurda and I got ashore, the boat and its grouchy owner disappeared. The staff led us through all these tunnels and caverns until we found the final piece – and you two."

Above their heads a mechanism popped open a hatch and they shot up into the open air. They bundled out quickly, and as soon as the cage was empty, the system of weights and pulleys yanked it back down. The grass-covered hatch slammed shut, concealing the secret entrance to the dwarfs' underground world.

They had surfaced in the middle of a range of low, bare hills dotted with rocks and dry gorse. Mount Daggerflash towered some miles beyond the hills.

"We should get out of here," said Lewis anxiously. "I don't like to think of those strange characters running around right under my feet."

"Yes," Sigurda agreed. "Haste is our best ally now."

So saying, she led the way westward with strides so long the youngsters could barely keep up.

They had not gone far when a hillside directly in front of them swung open like a huge garage door. A mob of dwarfs swarmed out, brandishing spears, swords and daggers, all of them chanting, "The dwarfs, the dwarfs, shall never be defeated!"

Fleebit was their leader and he pointed his sharp little sword at the intruders. "You have stolen our property," he accused, "so now, in payment, we will take all three of those magic sticks. Lay them down or face the wrath of the dwarfs."

The dwarf mob let out another cry of, "The dwarfs, the dwarfs, shall never be defeated!" to back up his demand.

It seemed to Lewis that they didn't have much choice. Small as the dwarfs were, they outnumbered the four of them by a good ten to one. He and Greg exchanged anxious glances with Susie, wondering what they should do. While they hesitated, Sigurda drew her sword and stepped boldly forward.

"Insolent wretches!" she roared at the dwarfs. "I am a warrior maid of Asgard, captain of the Valkyries, and I obey only the Lord Odin. If you stand in our path I shall mow you down like grass, and water the ground with your blood."

Fleebit turned pale and the whole dwarf host shrank back.

"You... you... can't talk to us like that," stammered Fleebit, struggling to recover his nerve. "It's completely irregular."

Behind him the other dwarfs nodded in agreement, though none of them looked minded to back him up.

Sigurda slashed the air with her sword and the dwarfs retreated with a whimper. "Return to your rat holes!" she commanded them.

The dwarfs began stumbling back to the open hillside, muttering fearfully among themselves.

"Sigurda," said Susie admiringly, "you are absolutely *EPIC!*"

"You know, Lewis, I think she's going to pull this off," said Greg.

As he nodded numbly in agreement, Lewis was suddenly aware of a shadow passing over them. He looked up just in time to see Falkior, Loki's great bird of prey, swooping down on them.

"Look out!" he cried, diving to the ground.

Sigurda started to turn, but too late. The giant bird's claws clamped around her arms and hoisted her helplessly into the sky.

"Sigurda!" Susie cried, reaching up after their friend.

Falkior climbed swiftly towards the clouds and they could see the Valkyrie struggling vainly in its iron grip. Vast wings beating the air, the great hawk flew eastward, back in the direction of St Andrews.

Lewis scrambled to his feet and watched the bird disappear into the distance with the helpless prisoner. The dwarfs too were staring up at the sky, stunned by the sudden appearance of the giant hawk.

"Right," said Fleebit, recovering his nerve, "now that the warrior maid has gone, we'll have our property." He started towards the three youngsters and the other dwarfs gathered behind him.

"Leave this to me," Greg told Lewis and Susie. "If Sigurda can scare them, so can I."

He stepped forward defiantly and waved the dwarfs away. "Right you lot, clear off," he said, "or I'll have the police on to you for disturbing the peace."

The dwarfs hesitated only for a moment then resumed their advance.

Greg raised a warning hand. "Think about what you're doing here," he cautioned them. "I've got a cousin in the SAS, two friends who are professional wrestlers, and I live next door to Iron Man."

The dwarfs pressed forward and the three youngsters backed off step by step.

"Well, I gave it my best shot," said Greg. "Anybody else got any ideas?"

The dwarfs were now in a very ugly mood, spurred on by their shame at how Sigurda had intimidated them.

"I don't think anything will stop them now," Lewis said.

Suddenly the dwarfs came to a complete standstill and started to shrink back. Lewis could see fear on their faces. All at once they howled in terror and fled back into the hillside, which crashed shut behind them with a boom.

"How about that!" Greg beamed. "It looks like my speech worked after all."

"I don't think so," said Lewis nervously. "I think there's something behind us."

"Lewis is right," said Susie. "Something's scared the living daylights out of them."

Very slowly the three of them turned to face whatever it was that had terrified the dwarfs.

Standing before them was the ugliest and most bizarre creature they had ever seen. It stood on six slim legs with a dark segmented shell covering its body and its long tail. It waved two huge claws and the antennae above its beady eyes twitched excitedly.

"What the...?" Greg gasped.

"It's a lobster," said Lewis, astonished, "a giant lobster!"

The lobster's mouth moved and they heard a familiar voice.

"Hi there, Elvis. It's really great to see you guys again."

"Dave!" Lewis exclaimed. "Is that you?"

"As sure as it always rains on a Scottish barbeque," said the lobster.

"Well, this is one for the books," said Greg. "What happened to you?"

"Look, I'm as curious as anybody," said Susie, "but shouldn't we get out of here before the dwarfs get their nerve back and decide they fancy shellfish for tea?"

"Right," said Greg. "Let's leg it."

Once they had put a couple of miles between

themselves and the dwarfs, they found a hollow among some rocks and sat down for a brief rest.

"Loki must have sent his pet budgie just to grab Sigurda," said Greg. "It didn't seem interested in the rest of us."

"What do you think he wants with her?" asked Lewis.

"I'm sure she'll be okay," said Susie. "Remember, Loki kind of has a thing for her."

Even while they talked about Sigurda, they were all staring at the lobster.

"Alright, Dave, maybe you should explain," said Lewis. "How did you turn into... *this?*"

The feelers at the sides of the lobster's mouth twitched as though it were trying to smile. "Yeah, funny story that," it said.

And Dave told them all about it.

# 20. A Lobster's Tale

Well, being attacked by a giant hawk while riding in a chariot pulled by a flying horse then plunging straight down into an icy pool isn't exactly my idea of a good time. Frankly, I've had better days. Lucky thing I'm an expert swimmer. Remind me to tell you about the time I went scuba diving in the Red Sea with my girlfriend Inga.

Anyway, I flounder around for a while, kind of shaken by the fall, but manage to get my head above water and catch a few breaths. I crawl onto land and find myself in the big forest that seems to have sprung up everywhere.

Well, I'm soaked through, so I find a clearing where the sun's shining. I take off my clobber and spread it out over a bush to dry in the sun. I reckon I should get a bit of shut-eye, so I curl up on a pile of leaves and doze off for a while. When I wake up I'm a bit groggy so it takes me a minute to realise somebody's speaking to me.

"Well, well, what have we got here?" says this voice, rough as sandpaper.

I look up and see, well, sort of a woman, but not really.

She's taller than me by a full head, and what a head. She's got skin like a mouldy orange and a hooked nose you could use for a tin opener. Her eyes are the colour of mud and her hair is green and stringy like seaweed. She's dressed in a grubby smock and she's wearing a necklace made of teeth and bird bones. She looks tough enough to walk through a brick wall and not even feel it. I reckon she's a giantess or an ogre or something else that isn't human.

Anyway, woman or monster, it's still pretty embarrassing that she's found me lying there starkers, so I take cover behind the bush.

"Sorry," I say. "You've caught me at a bit of a bad time."

"No need to be shy," she says.

I grab my gear and get dressed as fast as I can. Luckily it's mostly dried out while I was sleeping. I try not to goggle at her, but she is a sight.

"Here I was, gathering fungus," she says, waving a basket in one of her huge, wrinkled hands, "and what do I find? A little pet to play with."

"A pet?" I say, puzzled. "Oh, you mean me?"

I don't like the sound of this.

"My name's Dave," I tell her. "Very nearly Doctor Dave. I've still to finish up my thesis, but I'm sure it's in the bag."

She shakes her seaweed-covered head and says, "You gabble like a goblin with its foot in a trap."

I decide to shut up and not tell her how I've been studying lobsters for the past five years.

"My name's Gullygag," she says. "Maybe you've heard of me."

"Er, not that I can recall," I say, trying to be polite. "Are you a celebrity then?"

"I'm the most famous witch this side of the River Ifing," she says, sounding really proud of herself.

"That's cool," I tell her. "Do you get much hassle from the paparazzi?"

She laughs. It's not a nice laugh, though. It sounds like mud gurgling down a plug-hole. I laugh too, just to keep in with her.

"You use a lot of funny words," she says. "I like you. How about you come back to my place and I'll fix you a tasty treat?"

Well, I am feeling a bit peckish after all the excitement, so I say, "You're on, lady," and follow her through the woods. I reckon I'll get a bite to eat and then she'll give me directions back to town. Maybe she's even got a map. I mean what's the worst that could happen?

She's got a goat tethered to a tree close by. Not an ordinary goat mind. This one's as big as a horse. She unties it then climbs on its back, pulling me up behind her.

"I travel in style," she says with a big smile that shows off all three of her teeth.

Away goes the goat, galloping like the clappers. I don't know what she feeds it, but it's like riding on the back of a Formula One car. We whizz through the forest, trees flying past, rabbits diving out of the way for what seems like miles and miles. On the downside, this goat smells rank, so I'm not sorry when we reach the end of the line.

We get to her cottage, right, but it's not the sort of a place you'd want to go for a holiday. It's built out of rocks, mud, branches and stuff, with purple smoke coming out of the chimney. That's a bit fishy, I think. Not a marine-biology kind of fishy, but a really strange and a bit scary kind of fishy.

Now it looks bad on the outside, but inside it's even worse. There's animal skulls all over the walls and jars of weird-looking dust on the shelves, and whatever's burning in the fireplace stinks like dead mice dipped in pond scum or something.

"Take a seat," says Gullygag, showing me to a table covered in nasty stains, like somebody's spilt acid all over it.

I sit down, hoping against hope that the grub will turn out to be okay. Maybe a bacon sandwich or a lamb curry. Some hope!

She scuttles about for a bit then sticks a bowl in front of me. I'm guessing it's soup, but there's all kinds of muck floating around in it – rat-tails, nettles, toadstools, dead flies, moss, and other stuff I don't even want to think about.

"Get that down you," she urges. "It'll give you some pep."

More like give me food poisoning, I think, but I don't say it. Instead I manage to swallow a couple of spoonfuls and force a smile. "I've never tasted anything like it," I tell her truthfully, but not in the way she takes it.

"You'll want this too," she says, and tosses me a lump of bread that crashes down on the table like a rock. I try dipping it in the soup but even then it's so hard I nearly break a tooth on it.

I decide that the smart thing to do is to sweeten her up, so I nibble a bit off and say, "It's delicious. I don't suppose I could have a glass of water?"

She sloshes a wooden cup in a bucket and plonks

it down in front of me. The water's pretty grimy looking, but I drink some just to force the soup down.

By the time I've eaten half the soup it's getting dark outside, so I yawn and tell her I'm completely bushed and could do with a kip. She takes me to a tiny room at the back of the cottage that's got a bag full of straw on the floor. This is my bed she tells me, then goodnight, sleep tight and all that.

Well, after the day I've had, I doze off pretty sharpish. But the bad stuff's not over, even when I'm asleep. No, I have this dream where I'm a lobster floating in a tank of water and there's Gullygag's horrible face staring at me through the glass, like she's making up her mind whether or not to eat me. I wake up in a bit of a funk, I can tell you.

I get up and creep into the front room, thinking maybe I can sneak off before Gullygag wakes up, but no such luck. She's already up and about, laying some fresh fungus on the walls.

Soon as she spots me, she pipes up, "I've got all sorts of fun planned for today. We can hunt for poisonous toads, go for a swim in the swamp, then pick a fight with some bears."

"That all sounds great," I say, "but I've really got to be going. I don't want to miss the last bus."

185

She plants her knobbly knuckles on her big hips and scowls at me. "Going? You can't go. You're mine now. I found you."

"Sorry," I tell her, "I'm a one-girl guy and I've already got a girlfriend. Her name's Inga and she's from Denmark."

When she hears this Gullygag lets out a roar. "If she shows her face around here, I'll grind her bones into dust and use it to bake my bread!"

"That's a bit extreme, don't you think?" I say, trying to calm her down. "After all, we can still be friends."

"You're going to stay here with me," she insists. "I'll make you happy like that Inga never could. I'll make your dreams come true."

"If it's all the same to you, I'd rather you didn't," I say, edging towards the door. Then, quick as a flash, I'm out of there and running like the blazes.

Gullygag comes pelting after me with a bag in her hand. She's pretty quick but I'm a nimble sort of a guy and dodge around the trees, keeping clear of her. Finally she stops and chucks the bag at me. It hits me in the back and explodes in a shower of blue powder that covers me from head to foot.

"That will sort you out, you ungrateful worm!" I hear her yell.

Well, I don't stop running, I can tell you, not till my legs give out and I collapse in a patch of dandelions. I don't know if I'm just worn out from running or if it's something to do with the blue powder, but I fall right to sleep.

"When I wake up, well, I've turned into this. Yes, I've sometimes wondered what it's like to be a lobster, but I didn't want to find out in person. Did you know that lobsters can smell with their feet? I can't tell you how totally weird that feels."

"It looks like she really did make your dreams come true," said Greg.

"Well, the one about being a lobster, at least," said Susie.

The lobster's head drooped and its antennae dangled unhappily. "What's Inga going to say when she sees me like this? I'm pretty sure the wedding will be off, for a start."

"Look, we need to press on and rescue Odin," said Lewis. "I'll bet he can fix this."

"You think so?" said the lobster.

"Sure," said Greg. "He's king of the gods. He can do all kinds of stuff, you know, like a wizard."

The sun began to sink as they entered the foothills of Mount Daggerflash. The nearer they drew to their destination, the more they could feel the sections of the staff quivering. By the time they reached the foot of the mountain it was almost impossible to hold onto them.

"Maybe we should put them down now," Lewis suggested.

"Good plan," Susie agreed.

They laid the three sections of the staff end to end on the ground. All at once the magical runes glowed along the whole length of the wood and the three pieces fused together with a crackling sound, like electricity.

"That's quite a trick!" said the lobster.

"What do we do now?" asked Greg.

"I suppose we should pick it up," said Susie.

The moment she took hold of the staff the runes blazed like fireworks.

"Spinny, you'd better put it down," Greg warned.

"I can't," said Susie. "It's like my fingers are glued to it."

Suddenly the staff tilted so that it was pointing directly at Mount Daggerflash. A beam of light shot from the end of it and played over the mountainside. With a great grinding and creaking the rock face split open to form an archway, out of which stepped a tall figure, still wreathed in the shadows of the mountain's interior. The staff flew from Susie's fingers towards the man's upraised right hand, with which he grasped it firmly. Fresh light flared from the enchanted stick to illuminate the figure.

He wore a gold helmet and a black patch covered one eye. A white beard poured down over his silver tunic and a crimson cloak billowed behind him.

"Odin!" Lewis gasped.

# 21. The Eye of the Storm

"That guy looks a bit awesome," said the lobster, as the king of the gods strode towards them. "Are you sure he's on our side?"

"Don't worry, Dave," Lewis assured him. "We've met Odin before."

"Greg and Lewis, sons of Alan, and Susie, daughter of Theresa," Odin greeted them, "I thank you for restoring my staff and freeing me from this imprisoning mountain."

"Oh, it was nothing," said Greg with a shrug. "We're glad to help."

"But what manner of creature is this?" Odin asked, raising a quizzical eyebrow at the lobster.

"Dave the Lobster," said the creature, extending a friendly claw. "Pleased to meet you."

Odin glanced doubtfully at the claw.

"He's under some kind of a spell," said Greg.

"Yes, a witch turned him into a lobster," Lewis explained. "He's really a marine biologist."

"Almost a doctor of marine biology," the lobster added proudly.

"Such enchantment is only temporary and easily undone," said Odin.

He pointed his staff at the lobster, whose whole body began to shake. Its features blurred and gradually its claws turned into hands and its shellfish head changed back to the spiky-haired head of Dave the Lobster.

Dave looked down at his restored body and smiled broadly. "Well, that's a relief," he said, straightening his rumpled t-shirt. "I'm not sure I'll ever eat seafood again."

"But what has become of my shield-maiden Sigurda?" Odin enquired, raising his eyebrow.

"She was with us most of the way," Susie answered, "until she was snatched by that big hawk of Loki's."

"Ah, Falkior," said Odin. "He is ever ready to serve the cause of mischief."

"I expect Loki's holding her prisoner in St Andrews now," said Lewis.

"Yes, we must make haste to your town, torn from its rightful place by Loki to further his infamous ends," said Odin.

"It's a long walk, I can tell you that," said Greg.

"I have a swifter means of travel," said Odin.

There was an air of strength and wisdom about the

king of the gods that was immensely reassuring after all the dangers they had passed through. Lewis felt sure that Odin would manage whatever further hazards lay ahead and guide them back home to their parents.

Odin reached into a pouch that hung from his belt and pulled out a piece of wood about the size of a pencil. He laid it on the ground in front of him.

"What's this supposed to be?" asked Greg sceptically. "The world's smallest broomstick?"

Odin waved his hand over the stick and immediately it began to grow, unfolding into the likeness of a ship. It grew larger and larger, swelling up to the size of a lifeboat.

A mast shot up out of the deck and from it unfurled a golden sail, which rippled in the breeze. From its sides, where banks of oars would have been on a Viking longship, a pair of wings extended. They were made from green fabric stretched over a wooden frame, and slanted down so that their tips touched the ground.

"This is my ship, Skidbladnir," said Odin.

"A fold-up ship," said Susie. "Pretty neat."

"I could do with one of those," said Dave the Lobster. "You haven't got a spare one, have you?"

Odin walked up one of the wings onto the deck. He stood by the mast and beckoned the others to follow him.

"I'm not sure how much use this is on dry land," Greg mumbled.

As soon as they were all aboard, Skidbladnir began to move. The golden sail seemed to latch on to the air above and hoist them upward, while the wings began to beat, lifting them even higher. Floating above the surrounding hills, the boat pivoted eastward and flew off towards St Andrews. As they gathered height and speed, the landscape of Vanaheim rolled swiftly by beneath them.

The three youngsters gave Odin a brief account of their encounters with Loki and their journey to Mount Daggerflash.

"I knew at once what had given Loki this power," said Odin. "A splinter from the icy heart of Ymir, a foe I had thought long dead."

"This Emir sounds like a really bad dude," said Dave the Lobster.

"From what you have told me," said Odin, "Loki has broken his pact with the evil one and can no longer command the shard of Ymir's heart."

"The thing was running completely out of control," said Greg.

"Ymir himself must be guiding it from the depths of Ginnungagap," said Odin. "Still, all is not yet lost. Which of you has the Asgard crystal?"

"Crystal?" said Lewis. "What crystal?"

"The crystal in which the golden city of Asgard lies hidden, preserved from harm," said Odin. Seeing their blank faces he explained further. "When I saw that Loki was about to displace Asgard from Vanaheim, I used all the power in my staff to cast a protective spell over the city. It was shrunk to the size of my fist and encased inside a protective crystal. Moreover, the spell would cause the crystal to seek out one of the Ringwearers for safekeeping."

"That sounds great," said Greg, "but I haven't seen any crystal."

"Me neither," said Susie. "Sorry."

"We don't know anything about it," confirmed Lewis.

Odin shook his head grimly. "I know the spell did not go amiss. What can have happened?"

The lofty trees of Ironwood were rising up directly ahead and angry black clouds swirled and twisted in the sky above, as though stirred by an invisible spoon. The breeze was stiffening and they could see the trees bending before the wind.

"Looks like rough weather up ahead," said Greg.

"Is Loki doing it, do you think?" Lewis wondered.

Odin shook his head gravely. "It is Ymir asserting his power from the depths of Ginnungagap. This storm presages his coming."

The words were no sooner out of his mouth than Skidbladnir was jarred violently, as though it had slammed into a wall. The gale whipping through the treetops threw the little ship into a giddy spin.

"Whoa! This is worse than the Cyclone ride at the Lammas Fair!" said Greg.

The boat was tossed about in the storm like a top being spun by an angry child. Below them the treetops of Ironwood bent under the force of it and birds fled, shrieking, in a swirl of leaves and pine needles.

Odin placed a hand against the mast and gripped his staff in the other, using its power to control the ship as it fought its way through the tempest. Ahead they could see the spires of St Andrews illuminated by a lurid glow radiating from the town centre.

One corner of the sail snapped loose of its spar and flapped furiously while the wings bounced and cracked under the assault of the storm.

"Hold on tight," Odin cautioned. "We are almost through."

Suddenly the wind dwindled to a breeze and they glided across a peaceful sky, descending towards the outskirts of St Andrews.

"Phew, the wind's stopped blowing," said Susie.

"Yes, it's called the eye of the storm," said Lewis, "a calm area in the middle."

"Then why are we still wobbling?" asked Greg.

Dave the lobster peeked over the side. "Do you suppose it could be because the wings are coming off?"

They could all hear the creaking and cracking of the wings, which had been badly damaged by the gale.

"I shall guide us to a safe landing," said Odin as they glided over the outskirts of town.

"There's a clear spot there," said Susie, pointing. "There on Hallow Hill."

The ship dropped steeply and landed with a crash on top of the hill, just beyond the pair of Pictish graves that had been discovered there years before. The timbers cracked under the impact and the deck tilted abruptly, pitching everyone but Odin off their feet. The king of the gods stood unmoved, as though his boots were set in concrete, until the ship skidded to a halt beside a bent oak tree.

# 22. A Hole in the Sky

Everyone got to their feet and disembarked from the crashed ship. Lewis was glad to have solid ground under his feet again.

From their vantage point on top of the hill they gazed out over the town. From somewhere in the centre of Market Street a jet of light speared upward into the sky, piercing the dark clouds that swirled about it in a twisting waltz.

"I cannot face Ymir without first ensuring the safety of Asgard," said Odin. "We must discover what has become of the city of the gods."

"Mislaying a whole city," said Dave the Lobster ruefully. "There's definitely something fishy about that."

Greg's mouth opened wide, as though some brilliant thought had just occurred to him. "Fishy!" he exclaimed. "That's right, it's fishy!"

"Greg, I don't think this is a good time to be funny," Susie chided him.

"Have you conceived a clue to the whereabouts of Asgard, Greg, son of Alan?" Odin enquired.

"Look," Greg explained, "if this crystal had turned up in my pocket or something, I'd know about it. Same for Susie. But when this all started, Lewis wasn't wearing his ring; it was at home."

"You're right," said Susie.

"So what you're saying is..." Lewis began.

"The crystal was drawn to your ring," said Greg. "It's in your room, in your fish tank. Come on, Odin. We live just a few streets from here."

They hurried down the hill, headed for Bannock Street.

Susie suddenly peeled off towards her own house, which was close by in Rivermill Gardens.

"For heaven's sake, Spinny, what are you up to now?" demanded Greg.

"I'm nipping home to fetch my hockey stick," Susie called over her shoulder. "I'm not going up against a giant unarmed. Don't worry. I'll catch up."

As soon as they reached the McBride house, Greg raced upstairs to Lewis' bedroom. Odin, Lewis and Dave followed, heading straight for the fish tank.

"That's a first-class pair of *Carassius auratus* you've got there, Elvis," he said, casting his expert eye over Lewis' goldfish Ishmael and Ahab.

"Thanks, Dave," said Lewis as he peered into the water. Ishmael and Ahab stared back.

"Yes, I see a rock that wasn't there before," said Lewis.

He rolled up his sleeve and pulled out a crystal with a vein of gold running through its centre.

Odin's single grey eye flashed in delight as he took the crystal from Lewis. It immediately started to grow, but Odin fixed a concentrated stare upon it and it shrank back to the size of a tennis ball.

"Already the golden city strains to restore itself to its former size," he said, placing it carefully in a pocket of his cloak.

"So what do we do with it now?" asked Greg.

"Asgard cannot be restored," Odin replied gravely, "until the enchantments woven by Loki and Ymir have been undone and your town is transported back to Earth."

"We'd better catch up with Loki then," said Lewis, "before Ymir shows up."

As soon as they stepped out into the street Susie came whizzing down the road on roller skates. She pulled up beside them and proudly displayed her ice-hockey stick. "Now I'm ready for anything," she declared.

"We shall borrow this iron chariot," said Odin, walking over to Mr Larkin's Renault Mégane, which was parked on the street. He threw open the door and sat down behind the wheel with one arm out the window holding his staff. Greg, Dave and Susie piled into the back with the hockey stick laid across their knees.

"I don't suppose you have a driving licence?" said Lewis as he settled into the passenger seat beside the king of the gods.

"I don't believe so," said Odin, "but this vehicle will follow my commands regardless."

There was a flicker of light from the staff and the engine started up. The car roared off, guided through the streets by Odin's royal will. The town was still frozen into immobility, the whole population transformed into lifeless statues.

When they pulled into Market Street there were some familiar faces there to greet them. Kenny and Iona stepped into the road with their hands upraised in warning, prompting Odin to stop the car. Beyond the two police officers, Loki and Sigurda seemed to be having an argument at the base of a huge pillar of ice that was shooting a stream of baleful light into the clouds.

As they all got out of the car, Kenny said, "I'm afraid this road is closed due to circumstances beyond our control."

"Some normal people at last!" Iona greeted them. "Maybe one of you can explain what's going on here. I'm having a lot of trouble getting my head around it."

"Hey, you're not under Loki's control any more!" said Susie.

"I feel like I've been sleepwalking," said Iona, rubbing her brow. "I don't suppose anybody's got an aspirin?"

Odin's air of authority prompted Kenny to address him as though he were a chief inspector of police. "Sir, according to this gentleman," he said, indicating Loki, "a giant made of ice is about to emerge from that dimensional portal" – he pointed straight up at the hole in the clouds – "whereupon he will proceed to destroy every living thing in the entire universe."

Iona shifted her feet uncomfortably. "Kenny, you're making it all sound a bit far-fetched."

"I'm only reporting what he said," Kenny insisted.

"As you can see," said Loki, strolling over to the newcomers, "I've let them have their wits back."

"You've got some nerve, you creep, sending your bird to kidnap Sigurda," said Susie, shaking her hockey stick at him.

"You've got me all wrong," said Loki. "I brought her here to help me."

Sigurda came up beside him. "He wishes us to

be allies in the coming battle with Ymir," she said. "He seeks my aid in devising a common strategy."

"I've got to say, baby," Loki put in, "your plan that we should *die gloriously like the heroes of old* isn't exactly ringing my chimes."

"So where are the pet wolves that were supposed to be guarding you?" asked Greg.

"Those cowards!" said Loki disgustedly. "As soon as they scented what was coming, they took to the hills. Same with Falkior, the big chicken. I tell you, you really find out who your friends are when there's an evil giant on his way to destroy you."

"So that is the shard from Ymir's heart," said Odin, fixing a disapproving gaze on the enormous pillar of ice before them.

"It just grew and grew," said Loki. "It's completely out of control and there's nothing I can do to stop it."

Odin glowered at him. "Your selfish folly has unleashed the wrath of Ymir upon us all."

"Oh yeah?" said Loki defiantly. "Well maybe it's just a little bit your fault too for tossing me into that pit with him. What was I supposed to do? Spend all eternity letting him use me as a yo-yo? I had a chance to get out and I took it."

"I hate to admit it," Lewis murmured to Greg, "but he does have a point."

"There is no time for rancour," said Sigurda. "We must combine our forces for the coming struggle."

"Yeah, we can postpone the blame game till later," Loki agreed. "Assuming there is a later."

Suddenly a tremendous boom reverberated through the swirling clouds. Everyone looked up and Lewis' jaw went slack. A vast hole had opened up in the sky and beyond it they could see a dark, monstrous shape moving.

"Ymir is here," said Odin darkly. "The end is nigh."

Loki stared upward and swallowed hard. "You've got that right."

# 23. Slap Shot

Ymir's face was like that of an evil moon, harsh and craggy with eyes that smouldered like stirring volcanoes. Lewis couldn't bear to think how huge the giant must be.

"The fragment of his own frozen heart has opened a portal for Ymir," said Odin. "If he is to be stopped, we must neutralise the sorcerous energies of the shard."

"I'll give it another try," said Loki, hurrying over to the icy pillar and pressing both hands against it. "Come on you stupid lump of nastiness," he said through gritted teeth. "I command you to stop!"

When his order had no effect, Loki began slapping the shard in anger and frustration. To his shock, a blister of light suddenly swelled from the pillar and enveloped him in a shimmering bubble. Loki beat at the spherical prison with his fists as it floated into the air, carrying him up to where Ymir waited.

"I know he's a creep," said Greg, "but we can't just let that monster swallow him."

Lewis was surprised to find that he was also anxious to save the god of mischief. "You're right," he agreed. "There has to be some way to shut down the shard."

"The power of my staff may yet be great enough to do the deed," said Odin, striding towards the pillar.

He drew back his staff and swung, striking a mighty blow. There was a blinding flash and streaks of lightning crackled about him as magical energy flashed through the staff. Like an exploding glacier, the shard shattered under the impact. The detonation knocked Odin off his feet as the broken fragments rained down on the street, black and lifeless as lumps of coal. But the portal did not close up; Ymir's hideous face still glowered down towards them.

"Lord Odin!" Sigurda exclaimed, rushing to his side.

"Fear not," Odin assured her, rising to his feet. He looked weakened by the effort of destroying the shard and had to lean on his staff to stay upright. "What of Loki?"

Loki was still imprisoned in the translucent sphere, kicking the sides in panic as it carried him closer and closer to where Ymir was waiting to take his revenge.

"Look!" cried Susie.

Something else had appeared in the sky.

"Rimfaxi!" Sigurda exclaimed.

The winged horse swooped down towards them,

fully recovered from his injuries. He landed beside his mistress and lowered his wings to let her leap onto his back.

"Upward, my noble steed!" the Valkyrie commanded, grasping a handful of his glistening mane.

The horse launched himself into the air and Sigurda guided him in a steep climb, up and up, to where Loki was floating towards his doom.

Ymir's face loomed over them, his volcanic eyes boiling with hate.

Sigurda reached the sphere and smashed it with one blow of her sword. As Loki fell, she swooped under to catch him and he flopped face down over the horse's back.

Ymir's monstrous features contorted in anger and his mouth opened like a vast lunar canyon. A blast of poisonous breath poured out to envelop the Valkyrie as she sent the winged horse into a steep dive.

As soon as his hooves touched the ground Rimfaxi collapsed, desperately sucking clean air into his lungs. Sigurda and Loki dismounted unsteadily and stood coughing while the others gathered around them.

"Sigurda honey, that was pretty gutsy," said Loki. "Thanks a bundle."

"It was not right that even you should fall into the hands of one so evil," Sigurda replied stiffly. "Though I doubt you will prove worthy."

"You've got me wrong, sugar," said Loki. "When you've been trapped in a bottomless pit of nothingness with only an insane ice giant for company, it gives you a whole new perspective on things. I'm a different guy now."

"I hate to tell you this," said Susie, "but it doesn't show."

"Oh no! Look!" said Lewis.

Ymir had extended a colossal hand through the hole in the sky, and it was descending towards them with horrifying speed.

Lewis felt a cold terror clutch at his heart. "Won't the doorway shut now the shard has been destroyed?" he asked.

"It is too late!" Odin groaned. "The bulk of Ymir's body is holding the portal open."

"It's like he's got in the way of a lift door to keep it from closing," said Dave the Lobster.

Ymir's gigantic hand was pressing downward like a vast obsidian mountain.

"He's going to crush us like bugs," Greg gulped.

Sigurda stared up unflinchingly at the approaching menace, her sword at the ready.

It seemed to Lewis that normal weapons would be no use against such a colossal enemy, and Odin had drained the power of his staff in destroying the shard. What hope did they have left?

Suddenly Loki piped up, "Okay, he's got me mad now."

"What are you going to do?" asked Greg. "Call him names? Stick your tongue out at him?"

"Remember, I come from a race of fire giants," said Loki. "I'm going to fry him."

"I thought your fire powers were long gone?" said Lewis.

"There's still a spark, kid," said Loki, "that even a stint in the frozen dark of Ginnungagap couldn't snuff out."

Odin took a concerned step towards the god of mischief. "Loki, if you draw upon the very depths of your godly nature, you could die as easily as any mortal."

"I'm past caring about that, Pops," said Loki. "Now give me some room."

"Loki, as I saved your life, it belongs to me now," said Sigurda.

"Honey, when this is done you can cash in that debt whenever you like," Loki told her.

Lewis had never seen the god of mischief so determined. He was surprised to hear himself say, "Good luck, Loki."

"Stand back, squirt." Loki waved him away. "This is going to get nasty." He gritted his teeth and clenched his fists as streamers of fire began to flicker all over his body.

"Can I ask everyone to please retreat to a safe distance," said police officer Iona.

"Yes, this is a matter of public safety," said Kenny, as though they were keeping people back at a fireworks display on Bonfire Night.

Everyone pulled back into a wide circle as Loki's whole body glowed like the inside of a furnace. The town was now covered by the shadow of Ymir's descending hand and they could feel the air pressure increasing as the giant closed his grip.

Loki's face twisted in pain as the fire blossomed within him, burning up his own life force as fuel.

"Holy smoke!" said Dave the Lobster. "I think Logan is totally blowing his top!"

"I hate to tell you this, Ymir," Loki declared in a strangled voice, "but we're not pals any more!"

He raised his arms above his head and a torrent of fire blazed upward. The heat drove Lewis and the others even further back as the jet of flame blasted into the open palm of Ymir's colossal hand, burning a hole that belched steam into the air.

Ymir drew his hand back with a bellow of pain. Loki kept pouring on the fire until Ymir's whole arm had withdrawn into the far side of the portal. At that point the fire guttered out and Loki crumpled to the ground.

Sigurda rushed to his side. "Loki!" she moaned. "What sacrifice have you made?"

Even Odin bowed his head and wondered aloud, "Is this the end of Loki?"

Lewis' stomach sank and he could tell that Greg and Susie felt the same way. For all the trouble he had caused them, none of them had ever wished Loki dead.

Sigurda went down on one knee and placed a gentle hand on Loki's chest. For a few seconds everyone held their breath. Then, as if revived by her touch, Loki opened his eyes and sat up with a groan.

"Whoo!" he exclaimed. "That was a close one!"

Sigurda helped him to his feet. "Loki, you live!"

Loki nodded wearily. "But I've got nothing left. Baby, if we get out of this," he told her, "I'm swearing off magic for keeps. Maybe I'll open a restaurant or go into show business."

"Much as I'd like to make plans for the future too," said Dave the Lobster, "we still have a big problem."

The ghastly face of Ymir still filled the hole in space, and his cavernous mouth twisted in anger as he recovered from the blazing fury of Loki's attack.

"So all we have to do is get rid of that big ape," said Greg, "then switch Asgard and St Andrews back to normal. How hard can that be?"

"When Ymir is sucked back into the nothingness of Ginnungagap," said Odin, "all the harm that has been wrought by his icy heart will be undone. Both our worlds will be restored to their former state."

"Then we need to smack him in the face with something really big that will knock him right back down the hole he's climbing out of," said Greg.

"Like what?" said Dave the Lobster. "The moon?"

"That would be a bit of a tall order," said Susie.

"We do have something big," said Lewis. "Lord Odin, you have that Asgard crystal."

Intrigued by Lewis' words, Odin took the crystal out of his cloak so everyone could see it.

"So you used a spell of crystal protection," said Loki, impressed. "You've still got the moves, Pops."

"That's not what I'd call big," said Greg.

"Not now it isn't," said Lewis, "because the magic spell's made it small. But it was already trying to grow back to normal size. You can make it do that, can't you, Odin?"

The king of the gods nodded solemnly. "Yes, it would be a simple matter."

"So we shoot the crystal at Ymir," said Susie. "Then Odin has it snap back to its original size while it's in flight."

"You're talking about gubbing him in the face with a whole city," said Greg. "How cool is that!"

"It will be a shock for everybody in Asgard, won't it?" Susie worried.

"The preserving power of the crystal will linger long enough to keep them from harm," said Odin.

"Just one thing," said Dave the Lobster. "What are we going to fire it with? We don't seem to have a cannon handy."

"We don't need a cannon," said Susie. "We've got this." She raised her hockey stick in the air.

"Spinny, even you can't hit *that* hard," Greg objected.

"Remember the time Thor used his hammer to power up our skis so they could fly along by themselves?" Susie recalled. "I'm betting Odin could power up my Bearlander AX3 hockey stick to give it a cosmic wallop."

"That much magic remains in my staff," Odin affirmed. He gazed at Susie approvingly. "Susie, daughter of Theresa, you are a child of much wisdom." He handed the crystal over to her.

"I'm not so keen on the child part," said Susie, "but thanks anyway."

Odin laid his staff against the hockey stick and a shimmer of magical energy passed between them, infusing the stick with a brilliant amber glow.

Susie set the crystal down on the road in front of her then swung the stick right back so that its head was high above her shoulder. Her eyes fixed on the crystal and she wrinkled her nose in concentration as if she were about to take the most important penalty shot of her life. Greg could hear her murmuring intently to herself.

"Spinny, what are you mumbling about?" he asked.

"It never hurts to say a prayer, Greg," Susie replied without looking up.

Down came the stick in a ferocious swing. It struck the crystal with a concussion that shook the air like a thunderclap. The head of the stick flew up, completing its arc as the crystal shot into the sky.

"Kaboom!" Susie yelled in triumph as the gleaming gemstone rocketed towards its target like a guided missile.

Odin's eyes followed the Asgard crystal and he muttered an incantation to release it from its spell. Immediately Lewis could see the crystal grow larger, its facets multiplying by the thousands. As it expanded, the golden city inside sprouted domes and turrets and towers, unfolding into its true size.

Ymir slowly became aware of what was happening, and his vast eyes enlarged like blazing, poisonous pools overflowing with hate. The city grew and grew, still encased in the protective facets of the expanding crystal. It struck the ice giant square in the face with a boom that shook the ground beneath their feet.

Ymir let out a bestial roar that was a savage mix of anger and fear. The impact knocked him back like a powerful punch and he fell backwards into the Ginnungagap. The gaping crack in the sky closed in an instant with a deafening clang like an iron door slamming shut.

As the golden city of Asgard hovered among the clouds, the encasing crystal shattered completely. The tiny fragments drifted down in a rainbow shower that settled over the rooftops like light snow.

Lewis peered through the swirling, crystalline flakes, and felt the ground under his feet wobble like jelly. All the buildings around them wavered like reflections in rippling water. Up above, the air was filled with a golden radiance streaming from the city of Asgard.

As the effects of Loki and Ymir's magic were undone the universe shifted back into its proper shape. The town, the sky and the floating city of the gods all melted into a blur of blue and gold, then darkness fell, like the final instant of night before the start of a new day.

"Let true order be restored at last!" Odin's voice rang out. "Let peace reign once more over Vanaheim and Earth alike."

At his words a dawn of blazing gold broke across the sky, as though it were bursting from a thousand suns at once.

For a moment Lewis was blinded. When his eyes cleared, he found to his surprise that he was standing on the edge of St Andrews harbour with an empty glass jar in his hand.

# 24. Oddities and Endings

A Scottish barbeque is always a risky business, but this time the gamble had paid off. The sun shone down on the McBrides' back garden as everyone tucked into a feast of hamburgers and hot dogs with lashings of ketchup and brown sauce. Mrs McBride had even provided some tofu sausages in case any vegetarians showed up.

After yesterday's visit to Aunt Vivian, who had forced an Ecuadorian peanut and bean casserole on them, Mr and Mrs McBride had returned to St Andrews with a powerful yearning for some proper food – hence the impromptu barbeque they had organised the next day.

Susie's parents, George and Theresa, were there. George Spinetti brought along his latest batch of home brew to share with Mr McBride, while Theresa and Mrs McBride took a turn at flipping the next round of burgers.

Of all those enjoying the sunny afternoon, only Greg, Lewis and Susie had any recollection of the extraordinary events that had overtaken the town the day before.

"So yesterday turned out to be a normal day after all," said Greg, slurping on his huge tumbler of ginger beer and ice.

"Yes, once Ymir's power was destroyed, everything went back to the way it was," said Lewis, "right at the moment before Loki stole St Andrews."

"It was definitely weird finding ourselves back on the bus to Dundee," said Susie, "as though Sigurda, Odin, Ymir and all the rest of it had never happened."

"Well, I'm glad we made it to Dundee after all," said Greg, "or you would never have got to see my new thunder-splash dive into the pool at Olympia."

"It was pretty spectacular," Susie admitted, "but I'm sure they meant it when they said you'll be banned for life if you ever do it again."

"What a bunch of wimps!" said Greg.

Their attention was momentarily distracted by the loud snores of their friend Arthur 'the Chiz' Chisholm. Exhausted from the effort of wolfing down ten hotdogs in a row with scarcely a pause for breath, The Chiz had collapsed in a deckchair and dozed off. His deep slumber wasn't disturbed in the least by the yelling and screaming of Susie's two younger brothers as they raced around beyond the hedge, playing a game of Cosmic Warriors.

The back gate opened and in walked Dave the Lobster.

"Hi there, Elvis," Dave said breezily. "Thanks for the invitation. I hope it's for two because Inga flew in last night from Copenhagen."

Lewis expected Inga to be a tall, blonde Viking like Sigurda, but when she followed Dave into the garden she was less than five feet tall with short-cropped black hair. She wore a pair of coral earrings and a lobster claw necklace, which Lewis remembered was a gift from Dave.

"It is extremely groovy to be back in Scotland," said Inga with a bright smile. "I have been so missing your haggis and chips."

Once the introductions had been made, Dave accepted a bottle of George Spinetti's home brew and drew Lewis aside to a spot beside the garden shed.

"Elvis, I hardly like to mention this," he said, "but when I bumped into you at the harbour yesterday I was feeling a bit confused."

"I wondered why you left in such a hurry," said Lewis.

Dave shook his head, as though to clear it of a bad dream. "Even though it seems completely nuts, I had this notion in my head that it wasn't a normal day. That this guy Logan teleported the whole town into another dimension and we were almost destroyed by a giant climbing out of a black hole. I'm not going crackers, am I?"

"It's okay, Dave. I remember all that too," said Lewis reassuringly. "It really did happen. These rings we have and that amulet Inga gave you with Asgardian gold inside, they've kept us from forgetting it all."

"Well, that's a relief," said Dave the Lobster. He shook his head wonderingly. "It's a pretty wacky universe we live in."

"Tell you what, Dave," said Lewis, "it's probably best if we keep it to ourselves."

"Right," said Dave. "Mum's the word, eh?"

When Lewis rejoined his dad, Mr McBride was talking to Greg and Susie.

"I don't know why," Dad said, "but I feel we should be celebrating. Celebrating what, I don't know."

"Maybe the fact that we haven't been slaughtered by an insane ice giant climbing out of a bottomless pit at the end of the world," Greg suggested.

"Whatever you think you're talking about, Greg," said his father indulgently, "I suppose it's as good a reason as any."

"So, my young friends, you hold a feast in honour of our victory," said a familiar voice.

Lewis looked round and saw Odin had appeared as if from nowhere, dressed in a white suit and a Panama hat.

"Is this another one of your friends that you've invited along?" Mr McBride enquired affably.

"Oh, yes," said Lewis. "This is… Mr Owen."

"And what's this about a victory?" Dad asked.

"Ah, when Susie and I were at the pool yesterday," said Greg, "we got roped into a game of water polo."

"Mr Owen coached our team and we won," Susie chipped in.

"Yes, by two hundred points," Greg enthused. "Nice going, coach!" He offered Odin a high-five but the king of the gods did not recognise the gesture.

"Nice of you to come along at short notice, Mr Owen," said Susie, pulling Greg's hand down.

"I wanted to make sure you had all recovered from your heroic exertions in the… er… water-polo contest," said Odin, falling in with their story.

"Can I offer you a drink, Mr Owen?" asked Dad.

"Let me offer one to you," said Odin, pulling a bottle of golden liquid from his pocket. "I have brought a gift of the finest Asgardian mead."

"Very nice," said Dad, accepting it. "I'll go and fetch some glasses."

When Mr McBride had wandered off, Lewis said, "It's good to see you, Lord Odin. Is everything really back to normal?"

"It is as I told you," said Odin. "Once Ymir was

hurled back into the pit of nothingness, his evil magic was undone. Both Vanaheim and Earth have been restored to their former state."

"What happened to Loki?" Greg asked.

"Well," said Odin, "as you will recall, Sigurda saved his life. According to our custom Loki is compelled upon his honour to serve her for as long as she wishes. I have made him her shield-bearer, tasked with caring for her weapons and polishing her armour."

"I can't see him enjoying that much," said Susie.

Just then there came the sound of a musical car horn from the front of the house. "What's that? An ice-cream van?" Greg wondered.

Odin led the way through the house to the street, followed by Greg, Lewis and Susie. They saw that a red MG sports car had pulled up in front of their driveway. Loki was lounging in the passenger seat, wearing a straw hat and a short-sleeved shirt decorated with palm trees and pineapples.

Sigurda was at the wheel, but she looked very different without her helmet and armour. Her long blonde hair was tied back in a ponytail and she was dressed in a black t-shirt, a leather jacket and jeans.

"Loki, I thought you were supposed to be polishing armour or something?" said Lewis.

"Sigurda decided we should take a vacation," said

Loki airily, "check out a few places, you know, Paris, Rome, Venice."

"But as he is my servant, he, of course, carries the luggage," Sigurda added.

"That's a fantastic car," said Susie. "My Uncle Lorenzo drives an MG."

"It is no flying horse," said Sigurda, "but it serves well enough."

"Honey, I wish you'd let me drive for a while," said Loki. "I've always wanted to get my hands on one of these."

Sigurda slipped on a pair of aviator sunglasses. "I am in charge," she stated firmly. "I drive." She started the engine and flashed a smile. "Let us see what the world of mortals has to offer."

Loki waved as the car roared off and disappeared round the corner of Learmonth Place. "You know, Greg," said Susie, "we should go on a trip like that one day."

"Spinny, we just got back from the land of the gods," said Greg. "Let's take a wee break."

A brilliant pathway of multicoloured light appeared at Odin's feet and curved upward into the sky. Lewis recognised it as the Bifrost, the rainbow bridge that would transport him back to Asgard.

"I must return now to the golden city," said Odin. "There is trouble brewing among the Storm Giants."

Lewis glanced at the ring on his finger. "What about

these rings?" he asked. "Are they going to work any more magic?"

"You have no more need of such enchantments," said Odin, "for you have courage in your hearts. Those rings are mere souvenirs now. Never again will they blaze forth with Asgardian magic." He set one foot on the rainbow pathway, then paused and looked back with the faintest of smiles playing about his lips.

Just as he vanished they heard him say, "But you never know..."

# Author's Note

Many thanks to all the people without whom Lewis, Greg and Susie would never have made it out the front door. My wife and in-house editor Debby, who is always the first to read all my work and makes me try harder. My editors at Floris Books, Sally Polson and Sarah Stewart, whose suggestions helped to make these three books even better – and to all the team at Floris. My friend Jane Yolen, who prodded me into becoming a writer in the first place. And Diana Wynn Jones, the great children's writer, whose stories are clever, exciting and very funny, and who provided much of the inspiration for these adventures.

To find out all about me, my books, games and future projects, go to my website: www.harris-authors.com